**Lucy couldn't believe it.
These girls were trashing
her sister!**

"What a bunch of losers those girls are!" cried Lisa. "First they bomb out with their grades, and then they break into the gym and vandalize it. How stupid is that?"

"I know," Tina replied. "They made the whole school look bad."

Lucy slammed her locker and stepped up to the two girls. "Do you mind?" she said. "You're talking about my sister."

The girls exchanged glances. "Who's your sister?" Tina asked.

"Mary Camden," Lucy replied. "She was team captain."

Lisa looked at Tina, then back at Lucy. "Sorry," she said sincerely. "We didn't know. No offense to you or anything."

"Yeah," Tina said, nodding. "We *like* you."

Lisa chimed in. "You're not anything like your sister. You should come to the party with us!"

"Yeah!" Tina added. "But you know you can't bring your sister..."

7th Heaven™

SISTER TROUBLE

By Amanda Christie

Based on the hit TV series
created by Brenda Hampton

And based on the following episodes:

"Just You Wait and See"
Written by Linda Ptolemy
and
"Dirty Laundry"
Written by Elaine Arata

Random House 🏠 New York

All rights reserved under International and Pan-American
Copyright Conventions. Published in the United States by
Random House, Inc., New York, and simultaneously in Canada
by Random House of Canada Limited, Toronto.

www.randomhouse.com/kids

Library of Congress Catalog Card Number: 00-107441
ISBN: 0-375-81158-3

Printed in the United States of America
November 2000
10 9 8 7 6 5 4 3 2 1

RANDOM HOUSE and colophon are
registered trademarks of Random House, Inc.

CONTENTS

7th Heaven™

SISTER TROUBLE

CHAPTER ONE

WASH DAY

"I'm sorry, Matt, but I just don't think this is right!"

Shana's blond head peeked over the sacks of dirty laundry cradled in her arms. Her blue eyes were wide, her expression uncertain.

Matt, loaded down with an even larger bag of laundry, stumbled out of his black Camaro and kicked the door closed. Then he stepped around Shana to the back door of his family's house. As he fumbled in his pocket for the key, he leaned over and kissed her cheek.

Shana lifted her chin and stared at him. "Are you listening?"

"Yeah, yeah," Matt said. "Of course." He had just found the house key when his shoulder brushed the door. It swung open.

1

"See!" he said. "The door's not even locked."

Shana hung back, so Matt shrugged and stepped into the kitchen.

"I don't think it's right to drag our laundry over here," Shana said. But she followed him inside anyway.

"Don't worry about it," Matt called over his shoulder. "My mom doesn't care."

They plopped the sacks on the nearest counter, *then* they noticed Mrs. Camden standing in the corner, ironing shirts. She smiled at them.

Shana blushed.

"I *don't* care," Mrs. Camden said. "Really."

"That's very nice of you," Shana replied. "But you're already doing laundry for six kids and two adults, and I'm sure you don't need us dragging"—she pointed at the sacks—"all this over, too!"

"Don't be silly!" Mrs. Camden hung the last shirt on a hanger. "*Mi* washer/dryer *es su* washer/dryer."

She threw the shirts over her shoulder and headed upstairs. "I saved two pieces of fat-free cheesecake," she called down to them. "They're in the fridge."

Matt was already there.

"See," he said, pouring a glass of milk, "it really *is* okay."

But Shana frowned. "No, it's not! I don't feel right about this. I wish I hadn't agreed to it."

Matt closed the refrigerator and reached for Shana. She pushed him away just as Reverend Camden came through the back door.

Shana blushed again. Matt looked at her, then at his father.

"Hi," Reverend Camden said. "Doing the laundry?"

"Er...maybe," Matt replied. "If you're looking for Mom, she went upstairs."

"Thanks." Reverend Camden headed upstairs.

Shana turned and faced Matt. "I thought we were going to get together and talk tonight."

"That's what we're doing," Matt replied, moving closer. "We're here together..."

He slipped his arms around Shana's waist and pulled her to him. "Talking...washing... drying and..."

He leaned in to kiss her, but she pushed him away again.

"Matt," Shana said, wagging her finger,

"you can't talk me into it. It's just not going to happen."

But Matt's eyes twinkled and he hugged her. He was sure he could change her mind.

Behind them, Mary and Lucy padded down the stairs. When they overheard the conversation, they paused before making their presence known. Lucy was just about to clear her throat when Mary prodded her in the ribs and motioned for her to keep quiet.

Reluctantly, Lucy nodded, and they both listened.

"Look," Matt said softly, "all I'm asking is that you consider it."

"I have," Shana insisted, touching the tip of his nose with her finger. "So you can consider it considered, and the answer is no!"

"Okay!" Matt threw up his hands. "So you don't want pressure. Want to do a load of whites together?"

Shana looked away. "To tell you the truth, I don't want to do anything that personal right now."

On the stairway, Lucy's and Mary's eyes grew wide when they heard the word *personal*.

Suddenly, things seemed to be getting very interesting...

"Fine," Matt said. "You wash your whites first...*and I'll get Lucy and Mary off the stairway.*"

Mary winced and Lucy paled. Guiltily, they entered the kitchen. Without looking at Matt or Shana, they crept to the refrigerator. Lucy grabbed the handle.

"Don't even *think* about it!" Matt cried. "The cheesecake is ours."

Lucy closed the fridge.

"And anything you were snooping around to hear is none of your business."

Pushing Shana through the door, Matt grabbed the sacks and dragged them into the laundry room.

Lucy looked at Mary with raised eyebrows. Mary made a face. "It's none of your business," she said in an unkind imitation of Matt.

Lucy snickered.

Upstairs, Simon closed his book and sagged in his chair, the very picture of tortured angst. He felt crushed by the weight of the world. And the horrific ending to the sad book he'd just finished—S. E. Hinton's *The Outsiders*—only topped off his terrible mood. He sighed and rubbed his face with his hands. He almost felt like crying.

"Hey, what's wrong?" Ruthie said. "Are you going to cry or something?"

"No, I'm not going to cry," Simon said, recovering quickly. He laid the book on the desk next to his notebook.

"I'm...I'm *reflecting*. I just read this really terrible book."

Ruthie looked puzzled. "Why?"

Simon rolled his eyes. "Because I had to— for school. It's required."

"Why is reading terrible books required?" Ruthie said. "Do they run out of all the good books by the eighth grade?"

"It's not *bad*," Simon said. "It's just terribly sad. It's about people doing awful things. And at the end, Johnny dies after bravely rescuing these children from a fire."

Ruthie nodded sagely. "*That* will teach you not to play with matches."

"That's *not* what it'll teach you."

"So what does it teach you, then? Not to rescue other kids?"

"No…yes…well," Simon spluttered. Then he gave up. "The lesson is more complicated than that, and I don't have time to explain it all to you right now. I have a paper to write."

He turned his back on Ruthie and put his pen to paper. A moment later, he was scribbling furiously.

"Well…then…I guess you should get to your paper," Ruthie said with a sigh. She spun around and trudged back to her lonely room, Happy following on her heels.

When she got to the door, she turned and stopped the dog. "If you're coming in here, you have to dress for the tea party."

Happy whined. Then the little dog bolted down the steps.

"Go, you uncivilized brute," Ruthie said. "I'll just play by myself."

CHAPTER TWO

SUFFERING

The morning sun streaming through the kitchen window did little to lift Simon's spirits. The paper he had written about *The Outsiders* started him thinking about all the pain, suffering, and injustice in the world.

Then he found the morning paper.

A quick glance at the front page showed Simon that there were tragedies that he'd never imagined—and suffering in places he'd never even *heard* of.

How can I be happy when so many others are sad? How can I eat when so many go hungry? he wondered.

Simon knew he had to do something about the terrible plight the world was in. And he would start at breakfast!

A few moments later, Reverend Camden entered, adjusting his tie. He smiled at Simon, then blinked when he saw his son's meager breakfast.

"Ah," he said with an Irish lilt, "I see me boy is havin' himself a wee leprechaun of a meal. What happened to your eggs and juice, me lad?"

"Guilt happened," Simon said with a frown. "I can't enjoy my food when there are so many people in this world who are starving."

Reverend Camden blinked again. "Okay...," he said. "There *are* people in the world who are starving, and there are things we can do to help. But no one is going to be hungrier if you eat your usual breakfast."

But Simon wasn't having it. "It's a symbolic gesture. I want to remind myself of what's going on."

"So what is going on, according to the paper?"

Simon sighed and rattled the newspaper. Then he folded it to the front page. "Let's see, where do you want to start?" he asked.

Simon lifted the paper and showed his father the headlines. "How about the plight of the Kosovo refugees, or the famine in North Korea, or the kid who got caught stealing tuna fish at the 7-Eleven to feed his family—"

"Actually, that was his cat," Reverend Camden said. "The kid didn't want his mom to know he had taken in a stray cat."

Simon shrugged. "Do you know how many cans of tuna it'd take to feed all the stray cats in the world?"

"Hey," Reverend Camden said brightly, "I have some good news. Some of our parishioners got together and made a nice cash contribution that is really going to help the church."

"Why did they do that?" Simon said.

"Why not?"

Simon shook his head. "Because no matter how much money it is, it's never going to be enough to help everyone, is it?"

Reverend Camden opened his mouth to speak, but closed it again. He had no answer to Simon's question. There *was* no answer. And he also knew there was no way to help everyone.

Suddenly, Reverend Camden was feeling a little depressed himself.

*   *   *

"I have a gut feeling that Andrew Nayloss is going to ask me out," Lucy announced. She stopped fumbling through her closet and pulled out a pink blouse.

"Andrew Nayloss! The kid who lives in that big house right by the park? I'm impressed," said Mary.

"Nothing definite," Lucy added. "Just a feeling I have. So, if I go out with him, should I wear this?"

She held up the blouse. Mary made a face. "No, too teeny-bopper…I'd go with your new bold-in-black look. It's hot. And trendy. And you look really good in it."

"Thanks." Then Lucy smiled slyly. "What do you think Matt and Shana were talking about? Do you think when Matt said *personal*, he meant getting physical or something?"

Mary giggled. "I don't know." Then she caught herself. "I mean, *no!*" she cried. "Matt's *not* that kind of guy."

Mary grabbed a long black dress and yanked it out of the closet. "What about this?"

Lucy frowned. "It doesn't really do anything for me—and don't change the subject!"

Lucy took the dress and held it up. Then she

studied her reflection in the mirror and made a face.

"Do you think we should talk to him?" Lucy asked.

Mary looked horrified. "About what?"

"I don't know," Lucy said. "Just to express our opinions?"

"I don't *have* an opinion," Mary replied with a wave of her hand. "And I don't *want* to have any opinions."

"Don't you care?"

Mary sat down on her bed. "It's not that I don't care..." Her voice trailed off.

"Then what is it?" Lucy asked, sitting down next to her.

"I guess I'm not throwing stones because I've already had a million boulders tossed my way—with my grades going down the tubes, the trashing of the gym, and losing my scholarship and all."

Mary paused. "Plus, I'm living in the glass house of permanent restriction—the girl without a social life."

Lucy patted her shoulder. "I think Mom and Dad are going to ease up real soon," she said.

"It's been a while…plus the holidays are coming up."

"So what?" Mary sighed. "It's not going to make any difference. Even if Mom and Dad let me forget what I did, the rest of the school never will—thus, I'm the girl without a social life…"

Mary shrugged. "I don't care. It doesn't matter anyway," she said, less than truthfully. "There's no one to go out with and nowhere to go, anyway."

"It's been weeks," Lucy said. "The whole incident has been forgotten. No one is going to care anymore."

Mary looked at her doubtfully. "Are you kidding, Luce? It's never going to be forgotten. I'll forever be the Judas of Glenoak High."

Mary plopped down on the bed and turned her back on her sister. As the memory of her shame returned, so did her depression.

Mrs. Camden came out of the bathroom, drying her hair with a towel. She was shocked to see that the twins were crawling loose in the hallway.

Sam was rolling on the carpet and David was dangerously close to the stairs. Even worse, the plastic safety door was wide open.

"Ruthie!" Mrs. Camden cried angrily. "I thought you were keeping an eye on your brothers!"

Ruthie shot out of her room. "Oops," she said when she saw the twins.

"Sam and David are crawling now," Mrs. Camden explained, closing the safety door. "So that means they have to be watched every second."

Ruthie pushed the hair away from her face. Then she grabbed Sam, who was crawling quickly toward her room.

"I can't watch them *every* second," Ruthie protested. "The only one who can watch someone every second is God. So why don't we just let God watch them?"

Mrs. Camden was appalled.

"Because...because...," she faltered. "Because that's what He put everyone on earth for—to watch after each other. And I just don't understand your attitude!"

"I've got a big enough job just watching out

for myself," Ruthie said. There was defiance in her voice.

Mrs. Camden put her hands on her hips. "That's no excuse."

Ruthie shrugged, and she and Mrs. Camden carried the twins to their playpen.

"You have no idea what school is like these days," Ruthie continued. "It's every girl for herself. You can't be nice to everyone, and even if somebody could save people from a fire, he'd probably get hurt—even killed—doing it. And if you're just going to be killed, why even try to be a hero?"

Mrs. Camden took Ruthie aside. "How much sugar have you had today?"

Ruthie shook her head. "It's not sugar, Mom. It's Simon's terrible book. He was reading it and he got into a terrible mood, and he told me about it, and now I'm in a terrible mood. Do I have to read terrible books when I get to the eighth grade?"

"Never mind," Mrs. Camden said with a sigh. "Just help me get the twins back into their playpen."

Mary and Lucy came down from their bedroom in the attic. They were locked in an animated conversation and didn't notice Mrs. Camden coming out of the twins' bedroom.

"But he's got an apartment," Lucy said.

"And *she's* got an apartment," Mary replied. "So what?"

Lucy faced Mary. "So they've got the opportunity. And don't forget the motive..." She raised her eyebrows.

"A motive for what?" Mrs. Camden asked.

The girls jumped when they heard their mother's voice. Mrs. Camden cocked her head, but Mary and Lucy averted their eyes and remained silent.

Finally, Mrs. Camden shook her head. "We'll talk about this later," she informed them.

As Mary and Lucy retreated to the living room, Mrs. Camden peered into Simon's bedroom. He was ready for school and still reading the morning paper.

"That's certainly not going to cheer him up," she said.

CHAPTER THREE

TIME OUT

Mrs. Camden had fed the twins and dressed for the day. After she made sure Ruthie was ready for school, she went into Simon's room. He sat at his desk, his face creased with worry. He'd finished the newspaper and was rereading his book report.

"Excuse me, Simon, but what book are you reading? Ruthie said it was terrible."

Simon fished into his backpack and showed his mother the book.

"I think *The Outsiders* is a little over Ruthie's head," Mrs. Camden said. "How about steering her toward some of Laura Ingalls Wilder's books—you know, *Little House on the Prairie*? Something fun like that."

"Oh, yeah," Simon shot back. "Like living in a dirt house in the middle of nowhere is a barrel of fun. Then having your sister blinded by scarlet fever and then—"

"Okay!" Mrs. Camden cried. "Never mind. But I really think you could use something lighter to read yourself."

"Like these?" Simon replied, holding up the rest of the semester's required reading. Mrs. Camden glanced at the titles—*Les Misérables* by Victor Hugo, *Crime and Punishment* by Fyodor Dostoyevsky...

"Okay," she said. "So your English class is a little heavy right now, but how's history?"

"We're reading about the end of the Second World War and the invention of the atomic bomb," Simon replied. "And by the way, were there any good moments in history... *ever*?"

Mrs. Camden thought about it. "I can't say that humans have a very good track record," she said finally. "How about earth sciences? Isn't that fun?"

Simon shrugged. "We're studying the threat to our oceans and working on an experiment on global warming. Did you know that—"

"Math!" Mrs. Camden interrupted.

"That's my favorite subject," Simon said, smiling for the first time. "The answers are exact. Cold, hard numbers. I look forward to class."

Mrs. Camden smiled. "Math is the highlight of your day? Well, at least that's something."

"It's something," Simon said with a frown. "But it's not enough…"

Suddenly, Mary called from the living room: "The school bus is pulling out! Let's rock-and-roll."

Mrs. Camden patted Simon's shoulder. "We'll talk about this later," she said.

"Whatever." Simon rose.

She held out his backpack and Simon put his arms through the straps. Together they left the bedroom. Mrs. Camden tousled Simon's hair as he headed down the steps. He pulled away from his mother, a look of irritation on his face.

"Hey," Mrs. Camden whispered. "Lighten up!"

Simon rolled his eyes and disappeared down the stairs.

Mrs. Camden returned to the twins. She laughed out loud when she saw Sam and David peeking out from under their blanket.

"What are you doing?" Reverend Camden asked as he came through the door.

His wife smiled and pecked his cheek. "Just watching Sam and David," she said with a sigh. "They're so cute and innocent. I wish I could keep them that way forever."

"I know what you mean." Reverend Camden put his arm around her. "Too bad I don't have my camera—this is a Kodak moment."

Together, they watched their youngest children frolic. Then Reverend Camden checked his watch. "Gotta go," he said.

"So you're off to the church?"

Reverend Camden nodded. "I've got to work on my sermon. And I have some folks coming in later for spiritual counseling."

A frown crossed his face. "I've got a bad feeling about today," he announced.

"You haven't been talking to Simon, have you?" she asked.

He paused. "Well, actually, I *have*."

Mrs. Camden shook a finger at her husband. "*That's* your problem," she announced.

"The kid is a black hole. He's sucked the life out of the entire family with his foul mood."

Reverend Camden kissed her forehead and headed for the door. "I'll try to keep out of his gravitational pull," he said over his shoulder.

Matt's nose was buried in his textbook, even as he scribbled furiously on a well-thumbed notepad. When he heard the knock on his apartment door, he rose to answer it without looking up from the book. Matt opened the door and Shana entered.

"Hello?"

"Hold on," Matt said without looking up. "I'm almost there."

Shana waited, clutching a shirt in her hands. Finally, Matt closed the book and dropped it on his desk.

"I'm going to ace this test!" he announced with pride.

Shana handed him the shirt.

"I came over to give you this," she said. "It got mixed up in my laundry bag."

"Thanks," Matt said with a smile as he tried to put his arms around her. She eluded him.

"You didn't have to bring it over," Matt said. "I would have gotten it later."

Shana looked away. Her face was clouded with worry. "Later is something I'm not sure about," she said. "I'm...confused..."

Matt smiled, trying to ease the tension.

"And evidently, doing laundry together just confused you more."

Shana stared out the window, avoiding his eyes.

"What's wrong?" Matt said. "It's just laundry. Dirty laundry."

Shana turned to face him. Her face was blank.

"See," Matt said brightly. "This is exactly why we should just do what other couples do and..." He moved to hug her again, but Shana put her hand on his chest and stopped him.

"Matt," she said, her tone serious, "I think we should slow down."

"Slow down?" Matt was confused.

Shana nodded. "Slow down...and maybe see other people."

Matt's jaw dropped. "Where did this come from?" he demanded.

Shana turned away from him again.

"I think this relationship is too much for me," she explained. "It's…it's interfering with my studies."

"Right," Matt said doubtfully. "It's interfering so much that you have a 4.0 grade point average."

Shana spun around. "Yes," she said. "But I won't be able to keep up a 4.0 if this keeps up!"

"*This* what?"

Shana sighed. "This *relationship*," she said softly.

Matt's shoulders sagged. "Shana," he said, "I don't want to see other people. And do you know what? I don't think you really want to see other people for any other reason than to push me away."

When Shana spoke again, her eyes flashed with anger. "Oh, so you've already got it all figured out, don't you?"

"No, I don't have it all figured out," Matt said, angry now, too. "All I know is that I want this to work, and I would love to find out why you're being like this."

"Like what?" Shana demanded.

"Like distant and completely and unrelent-

ingly stubborn about something I want to do,"
Matt shot back.

Shana shook her head and moved to the
door. She couldn't handle Matt's anger right
now. Maybe she couldn't handle it ever again.
She just wasn't sure.

"I'm sorry," Matt called as Shana walked
out on him. "I've got this test, and…I'll call
you."

But Shana was already gone. Matt looked
down at the shirt in his hand.

"Hey!" he cried. "This isn't even my shirt…"

At Glenoak High, Lucy was dumping stuff into
her locker. She checked herself in the mirror
and decided Mary was right—she looked great
in black. But as Lucy prepared for her next
class—and applied some lipstick in case
Andrew Nayloss happened to walk by—she
overheard the conversation of two girls who
were standing nearby.

Lisa Morrell was tall, black, and regal. Tina
Gillis, a petite cheerleader, had straight brown
hair and always sported the most expensive
designer clothes. Both girls were very popular
with the boys at Glenoak.

"Have you heard?" Lisa said, gushing. "Janice just told me about the big homecoming party this weekend for the boys' basketball team."

Tina rolled her bright green eyes. "I can't believe you didn't hear about the party before this. Where have you been, girl? Only *everyone* at school is going. Everyone wants to show support after what happened with the girls' team."

Lisa made a face. "What a bunch of losers those girls are! First they bomb out with their grades, and then they break into the gym and vandalize it. How stupid is that?"

"I know," Tina replied. "They made the whole school look bad."

Lucy got angrier and angrier as the conversation continued. She didn't like to hear two of the most popular girls in school trashing Mary and her teammates. They had made a mistake, and they had paid for it. In Lucy's mind, that should have been enough.

But mostly Lucy was mad because she realized that what her sister had said that morning was true. Nobody at school seemed to be forgetting—or forgiving—Mary and her teammates for trashing the gym and embarrassing the school with their bad behavior.

"Weren't you just humiliated when the story hit the television news?" Lisa moaned with a frown.

Tina waved her hand. "Oh, tell me about it."

Lucy had had enough. She slammed her locker with a loud clang, then stepped up to the two girls.

"Do you mind?" she said. "You're talking about my sister."

The girls exchanged glances. "Who's your sister?" Tina asked.

"Mary Camden," Lucy replied. "She was team captain."

Lisa looked at Tina, then back at Lucy. "Sorry," she said sincerely. "We didn't know. No offense to you or anything."

"Yeah," Tina said, nodding. "We *like* you."

Lisa chimed in. "You're really nice, and smart, too. You're not anything like your sister. You should come to the party with us!"

"Yeah!" Tina added. "It'll be great." Then she lowered her voice. "But you know you can't bring your sister. No offense, but all the girl players are officially uninvited—they're *out*."

As much as Lucy wanted to go, she shook her head. "I don't think so," she told them. Tina and Lisa looked disappointed.

As she walked away, Lucy called over her shoulder, "No offense or anything."

They watched her go. Then Tina turned to Lisa. "Wow," she said. "Lucy looks great this year. Too bad she's got a total loser for a sister."

Just then, Mary came down the hall. She glanced at Lucy's locker, then spotted Tina and Lisa.

"Hey," she said with a smile. "Have you guys seen my sister, Lucy Camden?"

The two girls gave each other the Look, and then Tina pointed down the hall.

"She went that way," Tina said.

"Thanks!" Mary replied, taking off down the hall.

As she went, Mary heard the girls' laughter follow her. She turned and they stopped laughing. They smiled at Mary, then walked off.

Mary heard them laughing again, then Tina's voice floated back to her.

"That girl is *such* a loser..."

CHAPTER FOUR

THE ARGUMENT

As Lucy climbed down from the school bus, her friend Tammy called out a good-bye from the window. Lucy waved.

"See you at the homecoming party!" Tammy shouted as the bus pulled away in a cloud of exhaust smoke.

"Maybe," Lucy replied, waving. "Call me."

Then she turned and headed for the house. As she came through the kitchen door, Lucy checked the mail. There was still no sign of her driver's license.

It was taking an eternity to arrive! Lucy was tired of waiting.

Lucy's disappointment lifted when she realized what was really bothering her had nothing to do with her license. In truth, she was still steamed over her conversation with Lisa Morrell and Tina Gillis. She was bothered by the way they snubbed her sister, and troubled by her own feelings about the matter.

More than anything, Lucy wanted to go to that homecoming party. The invitation from Tina and Lisa, as rudely as it had been conveyed to her, was *so* tempting.

Everyone who was anyone would be at the party. Lucy knew it would be a lot of fun.

And why should I suffer because of Mary's mistakes, anyway? she wondered, even as she felt pangs of guilt for having such thoughts.

Lucy knew that snubbing Mary just wasn't right, but she was also secretly relieved that the whole school wasn't snubbing her, too. Yet she also knew she would be betraying Mary if she went to the party with the very people who were ostracizing her sister.

Lost in these gloomy thoughts, Lucy headed upstairs. As she walked down the hall to her room, Lucy spotted Simon cleaning out the drawers in his bedroom and throwing stuff into a big cardboard box.

"Are you moving out, too?" she asked.

"No," Simon replied as he tossed his baseball mitt into the box. "I'm giving these things away. I have too much—of everything. Material things just represent excess and waste."

Lucy stepped into the room and sat down at Simon's desk. She lifted the baseball mitt out of the box.

"You got this from Dad," she said. "Don't you want to keep it anymore?"

Simon sighed. "Everything I have is from Dad and Mom."

"I know," Lucy replied. "But don't you think you might regret giving away your baseball mitt someday?"

Simon took the glove out of Lucy's hand and tossed it back into the box.

"No," he said. "Because baseball is just entertainment, and people have spoiled even that part of the game. All the ballplayers and owners are just out there to make money. There's no loyalty to the game, to the team, or to the fans—especially the fans."

He paused and looked at Lucy. "I have no aspirations to become a professional baseball player," he announced.

Lucy frowned and threw up her hands.

Then, without another word, she climbed the stairs to her attic room and closed the door behind her.

Talking with Simon hadn't cheered her up at all!

Matt walked through the back door and proceeded directly to the refrigerator. He ignored Mrs. Camden, who stood rinsing the babies' bottles at the sink. Instead, he began to pile food into his arms—a Tupperware container full of chili, chicken wrapped in foil, lunch meat, milk, fruit.

When he couldn't carry any more, he moved to the table and sat down.

"Are you eating for two now?" Mrs. Camden asked.

Matt shoved a chicken leg into his mouth and chewed. "It's a high-energy day," he said between bites. "I had a big test and a big fight with Shana."

He continued to eat even as Mrs. Camden stared at him.

"She wants to see other people," Matt said finally. His mother gave him a look.

"No, Mom," he said. "I didn't do anything."

Mrs. Camden looked at him doubtfully. "What was the fight about, then?"

Matt got up and popped the chili into the microwave. "I don't feel comfortable talking about it right now," he said.

Matt closed his mouth when Lucy entered the kitchen. She crossed to the cupboard and grabbed a box of crackers. Then she looked at Matt and her mother.

"Don't worry," she said with a hint of sarcasm. "I'll eat these somewhere else so you two can talk. The conversation is probably too *personal* for me anyway."

Lucy turned to leave, but an angry Matt blocked her way.

"You know," he barked, "if I were still living here, you wouldn't have made that 'personal' comment in front of Mom."

Matt's furious tone made Lucy wince. She lowered her eyes. But Matt didn't let up and continued to press her.

"You're just trying to make me look bad in front of Mom because I didn't include you in a conversation about me and Shana that I've already told you is none of your business."

Matt's voice was loud and angry. Lucy

fought off tears as she bore the brunt of her brother's unexpected outburst.

Mrs. Camden touched her son's shoulder. "Matt?" she whispered.

"I'm...I'm sorry," Lucy gasped.

"It's too late," Matt shouted, unable to contain his anger any longer. "Ever since I moved out, everyone treats me like I'm some guy stopping by to eat or do laundry or something. I'm still part of this family, you know! And I'm still your big brother, which entitles me to lecture you." Matt shook his finger under Lucy's nose.

"So hear this," he said. "My private life is still my private life."

Lucy flew out of the room in tears. Matt stood in the middle of the kitchen, clenching his fists. Then he saw the shocked expression on his mother's face.

"I'm not apologizing to her," Matt said stubbornly.

"Okay," Mrs. Camden replied. "But maybe later you should *talk* to her."

"Fine!" Matt cried. "But her comment was totally uncalled for. My private life is my private life. End of story."

Just then, the microwave beeped, signaling that the chili was hot. Matt crossed the kitchen and retrieved the bowl.

"I understand how you feel," Mrs. Camden said. "But now that the word *personal* has reared its...interesting head, do you want to talk about your private life?"

"Not really," Matt said, plopping down at the table with the steaming bowl of chili in front of him. "I just want to eat."

"Oh...okay," Mrs. Camden said, still hovering over him.

Matt looked up at her. "I'll clean up when I'm done."

Mrs. Camden got her son's message. She picked up the babies' bottles and made a hasty exit.

"Matt's never yelled at me like that before," Lucy sobbed. She was sitting on her bed, crying on Mary's shoulder.

"It's no big deal," Mary whispered, patting her back.

"Well, it is to me," Lucy said. "He hurt my feelings."

Mary sighed. "Then you shouldn't have said

anything—like that word, *personal*. You were just trying to get Matt in trouble."

"Well, he was leaving me out of the conversation," Lucy protested.

Mary stood up and looked down at her sister. "You don't like being left out, do you?"

Lucy stopped sniffing and glared at her sister. "How would you know anything about being left out?" she demanded.

"I'm persona non grata," Mary said. "Or haven't you noticed?"

Lucy was suddenly uncomfortable with the direction of the conversation. But she wasn't going to back down, either.

"You've been part of the 'in' crowd your whole life," Lucy shot back. "You've been Miss Star Athlete, Miss Big Deal, Miss Popularity all during high school. You have no idea what it's like to be left out."

"Are you crazy?" Mary cried angrily. "Why do you think I got into basketball in the first place? I was like seven feet tall by the time I got into fifth grade. Kids laughed at me and called me names—so I did something. I learned a sport. I *used* my height instead of complaining about it."

Lucy tried to speak, but Mary continued her rant.

"I became an athlete instead of just whining about being different," she cried. "And after all that work, I'm nothing now. I'm just the tall bad girl who let everyone down, and now I'm paying for it."

Mary rose and headed for the door. She wore a frown and her shoulders sagged. Lucy moved to stop her, but the telephone rang.

It was Tammy, Lucy's friend.

"Oh, hi," Lucy said, trying her best to hide her emotion.

"So are you going to the homecoming party?" Tammy asked.

"No," Lucy replied, adding, "well, I don't know, really. I want to, but…"

"You've *got* to come!" Tammy insisted. "It won't be any fun without you. And lots of boys will be there—maybe even Andrew Nayloss! Everyone wants to show the boys' basketball team that they're loved and respected. Not like—"

But Tammy suddenly remembered who she was speaking to.

"You've got to come," she added.

"Let me think about it, okay?" Lucy replied.

"Sure," Tammy said, disappointment in her voice.

"Look, I've got to go," Lucy told her. "Bye."

When she hung up, Lucy sat down on the bed. Simon was depressed, Matt was mad at her, and now Mary was angry, too. And she couldn't even go to the party of the century because of her sister's criminal past.

Lucy sighed and shook her head. She had a lot to think about.

Matt had just finished washing the dishes and cleaning the countertop. As he worked, he fished into an almost-empty bag and stuffed Oreo cookies into his mouth. Simon entered and Matt offered him the bag.

"Go ahead and finish it off," Matt insisted. "There are only a couple cookies left."

"No thanks," Simon replied. "That's okay."

Matt looked at Simon. *Is this my little brother?*

Reverend Camden entered. He smiled as he reached into the bag. "Wouldn't want to let an Oreo go to waste," he said, drawing out the last cookies.

"Are you sure you can eat those, Dad?" Matt asked, patting his chest. "Your ticker and all…"

"Not to worry," Reverend Camden replied. "These are Reduced Fat Oreos."

He went to the refrigerator and poured himself a tall glass of nonfat milk. He was ready to take his first bite when Matt spoke to Simon.

"What's with you?" he said. "These are your favorite cookies."

"Not anymore," Simon replied. "Take a look at the ingredients on the back. Additives, preservatives, chemicals…it's all poison. And it's all because of money."

"Huh?" Matt scratched his head.

"All that junk is filler," Simon explained. "And the shelf life is probably a few hundred years. But what is it doing to our bodies?"

Reverend Camden set the cookie down.

"And I was looking forward to this, too," he said sadly.

"You may as well eat them," Simon declared. "We're all just pawns being manipulated by the corruption of politics and big business anyway."

"How do you figure?" Matt asked.

"Even though they know how the environment affects our health, corporations still make bigger gas-guzzling SUVs. They still package food in plastic that passes poisons into our bodies, sell weapons to other countries—then declare war on them because they used those weapons—and make paper towels and tissues that only promote waste and pollution."

With that, Simon stormed out of the kitchen. Reverend Camden looked down at his cookies. Matt glanced at the paper towel in his hand. Then they looked at each other.

"Don't ask me," Reverend Camden said. "It might have something to do with the fact that Deena's father caught her and Simon making out."

But Matt shook his head. "I think it's much worse than that," he declared. "I think Simon is learning the truth about the world."

"Come on, Matt," Reverend Camden said, punching his son's shoulder playfully. "It isn't *that* bad."

But Matt's frown only deepened. "Isn't it?" he asked.

Later on, Matt went to the dryer and grabbed

some clothes he'd washed earlier. He thought about Shana and her wish to see other people. He still didn't think she wanted that. And he *knew* that was not what he wanted.

But lately, Matt's desires hadn't counted for much—not with Shana. Not with his own family.

He was finished bagging his clothes and was heading for the front door when Mary bounded down the stairs.

"Hey," Mary said.

"Just to let you know," Matt told her, "Shana and I had a fight, so you can tell Lucy all about it. I'm sure she's dying to know."

"Look," Mary replied, "I'm not your messenger and I don't care what you and Shana are doing."

"Oh, right, I forgot," Matt retorted. "You don't care about anyone but yourself."

Before a stunned Mary could reply, Matt spun around and walked out the door. It slammed behind him.

Well, now I know how Lucy felt, Mary thought. *Matt really knows how to hurt a girl when she's down....*

Then Mary kicked the door Matt had just walked through.

What is wrong with this family, anyway?

"Hey, Matt," called John Hamilton, Matt's college roomate. "My man is finally home."

John emerged from the bathroom. He was all smiles.

"Guess you did well on your test," Matt said, plopping down on a well-worn couch.

John gave him up a double thumbs-up. "Aced it. How about you?"

"Aced it," Matt said with a distracted half smile.

John looked at him. "Thank goodness you didn't flunk it—you might have killed yourself by now. You don't look like a man who aced the big test. What's wrong?"

"Nothing," Matt lied.

"Does that nothing have something to do with Shana?"

"Look, I don't want to talk about it, and it has nothing to do with Shana."

"Okay, okay," John said. "I'm on my way to meet Bobby and Tilman—we're going to see that new Mel Gibson movie. Do you want to come? Students get in half-price."

"That's okay. I'll pass."

"Well, I've got to go," John said, grabbing his jacket. "See you later."

John paused at the door. "By the way," he said, "if that *it* thing that's not wrong and has nothing to do with Shana *is* wrong and *is* about Shana, then you might want to listen to the message on the answering machine."

Then he was out the door.

Matt got up and looked at the blinking light. Then he touched the button.

"Hi, this is Shana, for Matt...Matt, listen. I'm really sorry about today...I don't really want to see other people..."

Matt put his hands above his head and danced in a circle. *Yes! She's finally come to her senses.*

"...but I do want a time-out from you. I'll call you."

Stunned, Matt fell back onto the couch. *Time-out? From me?*

CHAPTER FIVE

LIGHTEN UP

As Mrs. Camden carried a basket of freshly laundered clothes up the stairs, she overheard Simon commiserating with his dog, Happy.

"It's just another day," he sighed. "Another day of gray walls, pointless lessons, and chalk dust."

Mrs. Camden shook her head. This black mood of Simon's had to end.

"How are you doing?" Mrs. Camden asked, stepping into Simon's room.

"Oh, okay," he replied. "Considering."

He looked down at the newspaper cradled in his lap. A terrible car crash was pictured on the front page in vivid color. Mrs. Camden snatched the newspaper out of his hand. Surprised, Simon looked up.

"Yes," she replied brightly. "I'm okay, too. Considering this bad mood of yours has set off a bad mood with practically every member of the family."

"I'm sorry," Simon replied. "I didn't know anyone else was in a bad mood."

"That's part of the problem," Mrs. Camden said, sitting down in a chair. "You're so wrapped up in your own bad mood you don't even notice anyone else."

Simon thought about it.

"You have to stop," his mother insisted. "Bad moods are as contagious as chicken pox."

"Yeah, well, it seems the whole world is in a bad mood," Simon said, pointing to the newspaper in his mother's hand.

She stood up again. "You know, good moods are contagious, too," she said. "So, as of right now, we both are going to be in a better mood."

Simon rolled his eyes. "Oh, just like *that*."

"Yes. Exactly," Mrs. Camden replied brightly. "Just like that. All it takes is an act of will. You *do* believe in free will, don't you?"

Simon nodded.

"Good! We're going to put on a smile and pretend to be in a good mood."

Simon's eyebrow went up. "You mean fake it?"

"What's the difference between pretending to be in a good mood and being in a good mood?" she asked.

"You got me," Simon said with a shrug.

"It's actually very hard to tell the difference," Mrs. Camden said. "So just start by pretending, and the reality will catch up with you."

Simon made a face. "I'll try it," he said. "But I don't know how long it's going to last."

Mrs. Camden leaned down and whispered in Simon's ear.

"I know how to *make* it last," she said. "Once you get your mood up, help someone actually do something that contributes to someone *else* feeling better, or getting what *they* need."

Simon nodded, seeing the logic.

Mrs. Camden winked. "Service to others makes *you* feel good."

But Simon sighed. "There are so many others to serve."

"That's right!" Mrs. Camden said. "So pick one. And another. And another one after that..."

She tousled his hair. "And smile, baby, smile!"

Mrs. Camden smiled at her son. With an effort, he managed to smile back to her. She gave him a thumbs-up.

As she marched out of Simon's room, Mrs. Camden tossed the newspaper in the trash can.

All the next morning at school, Lucy had managed to avoid talking to Tammy. She still didn't want to commit to the party, but she didn't want to say no, either. Lucy was still torn between doing what she thought was right, and doing what she really wanted. Until she resolved that dilemma, Lucy wanted to keep her options open.

But when she arrived at her locker before lunch break, Lucy found Tina Gillis and Lisa Morrell waiting for her.

"Hey, Lucy," Tina said. "Are you sure you don't want to come to the party? Darrell Tyson and Brad Bateson are both coming."

"And Andrew Nayloss might be there, too,"

Lisa whispered. "I heard that he likes you."

Lucy's heart skipped a beat. "Really?" she said, hiding her excitement. *Let it be true! Let it be true!*

"That's what we've heard," Lisa said. "And we think you really ought to come."

"Tammy told us you still hadn't made up your mind," Tina added. "Come on, it'll be fun."

"Well…" Lucy thought about it. Tina and Lisa exchanged excited glances.

Just then, Mary came down the hall. As she approached the group, Tina and Lisa looked away.

"Hey, Luce," Mary said. "Do you have a second?"

"Sure," Lucy said, stepping away from her friends.

"Look," Mary began, "I'm sorry about last night. You were crying and I was just mean to you. And this is my problem, not yours."

"Problem?"

"Never mind," Mary said with a wave. "It's probably all in my head that people are shunning me and the other basketball players, anyway."

Tina and Lisa overheard Mary's remark.

They giggled and walked away. Lucy waved nervously as they said good-bye to her.

"Okay," Mary said. "Maybe people really are shunning me. But it's got to blow over eventually, right?"

"Er, right!" Lucy replied nervously.

"And even if it doesn't," Mary continued, "at least I've got my family."

"Yeah…"

Just then, Tammy walked past. "Hey, Luce," she called. "I was just talking to Lisa and Tina—they said you were coming to the homecoming party. See you on Saturday night!"

Tammy shook her fist above her head as she headed for the next class, chanting, "Par-ty! Par-ty! Par-ty!"

Mary stared at Lucy.

"I—I wasn't going to go!" Lucy stammered. "Then…then I thought I *might* go. I mean, it's not like *I* got in trouble, right?"

"Right," Mary said with an angry nod. "You did nothing. Nothing except join a whole group of people who are deliberately excluding me!"

As Mary stormed down the hall, Lucy banged her head against the locker over and over again.

* * *

Matt entered the house through the back door. He found his mother just where he thought she'd be—making dinner. She looked up from the pile of potatoes she'd been peeling when he came in. When she saw him, she went back to work. Matt could tell she was still upset over the way he had treated Lucy and Mary and the way he shut her out of his problems—even though all she wanted to do was help.

"Okay," Matt said. "If you want to know so badly, I'll tell you what Shana and I were talking about."

Mrs. Camden smiled, dropped the potato peeler, and dried her hands. Then she offered Matt a chair.

"Talk to me," she said.

Matt sat down and took a deep breath. "Shana and I started having some...problems. We couldn't talk about them, so I talked to John about them."

Mrs. Camden nodded.

"Then Shana got mad because I talked to John," he continued. "So I suggested that we both go and talk to someone else together.

Someone like a counselor. They have counselors on campus."

"That sounds reasonable," Mrs. Camden agreed.

"Yeah," Matt said. "I thought so, too. Especially since Shana already sees a therapist and Dad helped her and her brother. It wasn't like I was suggesting something for the two of us that she doesn't already do for herself."

He paused, recalling the scene. "But she *flipped*. She refuses to go and she refuses to talk about whatever it is that's bothering her."

Mrs. Camden thought about it for a moment.

"Do you think Shana would want to talk to me?" she asked.

Matt shrugged. "Maybe," he said. "She's not close to her own mom."

"Maybe I'll call her and ask if she has time to come by and not make it any big deal."

Matt nodded reluctantly. But he didn't look okay with the idea.

Mrs. Camden finished peeling potatoes and asked Matt to stay for dinner. He agreed, as long as he could work for his meal. So she sent him off to pick up the dry cleaning.

She was reaching for the telephone to call Shana when it rang. Mrs. Camden answered it.

"Hi, this is Shana," the voice on the other end of the line said shyly. "I know I have no right to ask this, but...could I come over and talk to you tomorrow?"

"Of course!" Mrs. Camden said with a triumphant smile.

And I didn't even have to ask....

CHAPTER SIX

THE CONVERSATION

Mary heard the knock on her door and chose to ignore it. There was a second knock, and Simon thrust his head through the door. Mary saw him and turned back to the homework on her desk. Simon came in and sat down on the bed, watching her. Finally, Mary plunked down her pencil and faced her brother

"Why bother knocking? Since you've already decided to come in."

Simon shrugged. "I guess I thought it was the polite thing to do."

"No," Mary said. "The polite thing to do is to wait until the occupant—that would be *me*—gives the visitor—that would be *you*—actual permission to enter."

"Okay," Simon said with a smile. He

jumped to his feet, went out the door, then knocked again.

"Go away!"

Simon came in anyway. Mary rolled her eyes.

"If you're trying to irritate me, you can go now, because you have accomplished your mission."

But Simon sat down on the bed again. His smile was really starting to get to her.

"Look," he said, "I actually want to help you. Out of seven family members, you're definitely the worst off."

Mary raised her eyebrow. "Oh, really?"

Simon nodded.

"Well, there's nothing you could do that could possibly help me out," Mary declared. "So bye-bye."

"I can at least get you in a better mood," Simon said.

"I don't think so," Mary replied. "But you *could* close the door on the way out."

She picked up her pencil and began to work. Simon rose and began to sing in a Caribbean lilt.

"Don't worry...be happy..."

He accompanied his solo with a little soft-shoe shuffle. Mary chuckled in spite of herself as Simon danced around the attic room. Then she rose and shooed him out the door. He sang and danced the whole way. Even when she closed the door behind Simon, she could hear him singing and dancing down the steps and along the hallway.

What is wrong with this family? Mary wondered again. But this time, she was smiling.

Simon was still singing and dancing up and down the hall when he bumped into Lucy. She stared at him as if he was deranged.

"What happened to Mr. Doom and Gloom?"

Simon kicked up his heels and did a quick spin. Then he took Lucy's hands in his and spun her around, too.

"I'm not raining on anyone's parade," he told her. "I'm a new man. A *happy* man!"

Simon spun Lucy again, then pushed her away. He began to dance all around her—a little bit of tango, with a touch of *Saturday Night Fever* disco inferno.

Lucy watched him, making a frown. "Lucky you," she said. "I'd love to be a happy woman."

"That's just it!" Simon cried. "You can!"

Lucy gave him a look that asked "How?"

Simon paused. "There's a clothing drive at my school for the Kosovo refugees. Maybe you could get some things together for me to take tomorrow. It would help a lot of people who need help pretty badly."

Lucy didn't even have to think about it. "Okay," she said. "I've got stuff I'm never going to wear again. Including a teeny-bopper blouse that Mary says is too young for me."

"Then go, Miss Lucy, go!"

As Lucy headed off to her room, Simon began to dance again, but this time he put his hips into it. Soon he was doing a fair impression of Elvis. He snatched a candleholder from the hall table and used it for a microphone.

"I'm in love—I'm all shook up!" Suddenly, Simon was dancing and twisting and throwing his head around as he sang the rest of his favorite Elvis song.

The door to Ruthie's bedroom burst open and she came storming out.

"What's with all the racket?" she demanded. "I've got the blues and I don't want to be disturbed. And you're making too much noise!"

Simon danced right up to her.

"The blues are good, but a good mood's even better," he declared.

Ruthie snorted.

"Really," said Simon. "It has sort of a healing quality about it."

"Right," Ruthie replied, turning away.

"You should try it." Simon spun his little sister around. Ruthie struggled against him, but he held her tightly.

"You could get into a good mood, too!" he said. But Ruthie still struggled.

"No, I can't!" she screamed.

But Simon wouldn't have it. He spun Ruthie again until she was facing him. Then he gripped her shoulders and held her in place.

"Admit it!" he said. "You're not really enjoying the blues, are you?"

Ruthie stopped fighting and thought about it for a minute. "No, not really," she said after a long pause.

"Okay, then." Simon released her. "Then get up, do something, help someone..." Simon began to make a song of it.

"Get up...do something...help someone who needs you..."

Ruthie tugged on his sleeve. "Help who?" she said. "I don't have any friends."

Simon smiled and danced in a circle around her. "Then, my child, you must go out and find friends—*make* friends...."

As he danced away from her and down the stairs, Ruthie watched him. She couldn't help but laugh.

And suddenly, her blues had disappeared.

In the laundry room, Mrs. Camden and Shana were folding clothes together. The twins were in the playpen, dozing. The room was quiet, and the two women worked in silence. Shana would pause to take a sip of her iced tea, or simply to stare off into space. Mrs. Camden waited patiently for her to speak.

Shana sighed loudly.

"Is it me, or is it awkward in here?" Mrs. Camden said at last.

Shana smiled shyly, then nodded.

"It's awkward in here," she said with a laugh. Then she was silent. Mrs. Camden folded more clothes and glanced at the twins. They were sound asleep.

"I came over to talk," Shana said. "I *want* to talk. I called you because I wanted to talk. But I don't know how to talk."

Mrs. Camden smiled. "Yet here we are...talking."

"What do you know?" Shana said with a nervous smile.

"Well, I know a little something," Mrs. Camden continued. "I know that Matt offended you by talking to John about your personal problems."

"Yet he can't talk to *me* about me," Shana said.

"And you don't want to get into counseling with him."

Shana nodded. She opened her mouth to speak, but then turned her eyes away and said nothing.

Mrs. Camden reached out and patted her arm.

"Well, maybe it's not that serious," she said. "Maybe you don't need a professional. Maybe all you need is a friend...or a mom?"

Shana blushed. Then she spoke, and it was like opening the closet in Ruthie's bedroom—everything came tumbling out.

"The thing is, it *is* serious," Shana began. "I have a *serious* problem. And there are two kinds of people in the world—those who have seen a therapist, and those who haven't. I'm the first. Matt's the second."

Shana faced Mrs. Camden.

"I...I just don't want to air my dirty laundry in front of Matt," Shana said. "We're close, but not that close—not yet. Maybe not ever. And I'd like to know how close we're going to get before I reveal everything about myself—including the bad stuff. And the *really* bad stuff..."

"What about your own mom?" Mrs. Camden asked.

Shana shook her head. "I can't air my dirty laundry in front of my mom because my mom *is* my dirty laundry. My therapist knows that, but Matt doesn't."

Shana faced Mrs. Camden. Her eyes were moist, but she couldn't stop the words that poured out of her.

"I had a crummy life, but the crummy part is over. I've grown up and I'm on my own and I'm doing fine. But I didn't grow up like a normal person, and I don't even know how to do the simplest things like normal people."

"What do so-called normal people do?" Mrs. Camden asked.

"Simple things—like laundry," Shana replied. "To me, laundry seems so personal. Putting your dirty stuff in with someone else's dirty stuff—is that okay?"

Mrs. Camden opened her mouth to speak, but Shana ran right over her.

"Putting my dirty underwear in with Matt's dirty underwear when we've never even seen each other's underwear—is that okay? Or is it weird? What do normal girlfriends and boyfriends do when they do laundry together? I don't know, 'cause I'm not normal."

Mrs. Camden didn't try to respond anymore. She just let Shana talk, because that was what she needed to do.

"I know it sounds stupid not knowing what normal people do, but I don't. I'm embarrassed, or I would be, but..."

Then Shana began to laugh.

"This is insane!" she cried, bopping herself on the head. "I don't *care* about how other people do their laundry. My goal isn't to be normal—my goal is to be me."

Shana looked into Mrs. Camden's eyes.

"I guess that's what I've been so afraid of talking about with Matt," she said softly. "And I guess that's what I'm going to have to tell him."

Then Shana threw her arms around Mrs. Camden and pulled her close.

"I'm sorry," she said. "I guess I needed to work all of that out by saying it out loud."

Shana squeezed Mrs. Camden even tighter.

"Thanks...thank you so much for listening," she said softly, smiling now. Mrs. Camden grinned and hugged Shana back.

CHAPTER SEVEN

DIRTY LAUNDRY

Matt worked his afternoon shift at the hospital cafeteria, then headed straight for the Camden home. He figured John was still out with his friends, and Matt couldn't bear to face an empty apartment—not in the foul mood he was in. He needed the comfort of family, even if they were mostly mad at him.

He pulled his Camaro in to the driveway and climbed out. The house was quiet, but the kitchen light was on. Matt let himself in and discovered the kitchen was empty. He made himself a snack—real food, not hospital food—and wolfed it down.

Matt sniffed his uniform and decided to wash it. He went into the laundry room and found his sweatpants and T-shirts washed and folded and waiting for him next to a huge stack of clean towels.

Matt changed and tossed his uniform into the washer. Then he loaded up an empty basket with clean laundry and took it upstairs.

Matt opened the hall closet and began to stack up towels. He heard a door open behind him but didn't turn around.

He felt a slap on his back.

"Hey, big brother," Simon said with a grin. "You know, it's nice having you still come around so much. Want some help with that?"

Matt looked at Simon, then looked around. "Am I in the right house?"

"Ha, ha!" Simon chuckled. "That's funny, Matt. Of course you're in the right house. It's your house, too! And we're your family, brother."

"Well, thanks," Matt said finally. "But that's okay, I don't need help. I'm just cleaning up for Mom."

"Okay, brother mine," Simon chirped. Then he danced down the steps. Matt shook his head, wondering what had happened to Simon "Doom and Gloom" Camden.

Matt stooped down, rearranging the towels

to make room for the clean ones. As he worked, he felt something tug on the clothes tucked under his arm. A moment later, the whole load tumbled to the floor.

"I'm sorry," Lucy said, blushing. "I just wanted my jeans. I didn't mean to knock everything over and make a mess."

"No, I'm sorry," Matt replied. "I didn't see you coming, or I would have handed them to you."

They both scrambled on the hall carpet for the fallen clothes. Then their eyes met. Lucy dropped the clothes in her hand and hugged Matt.

"I hate it when you're mad at me," she said, fighting back tears.

"I know," Matt said, hugging her back. "I feel just as bad when you're mad at me."

They hugged in silence, then Matt spoke.

"I got upset because when I said the word *personal*, everyone just assumed that Shana and I were talking about kissing and stuff," Matt explained. "But really, we weren't. Not that that's anyone's business anyway."

Lucy blinked, surprised.

"I know it's not my business," she said. "But

you *were* doing laundry together."

"So?"

"Are you kidding?" Lucy cried. "I can't believe you're so dense."

Matt was really puzzled now. "What are you talking about?"

"Goodness, Matt," Lucy continued. "I'd have to be practically *married* to let some guy see my dirty clothes. Yuck."

Matt bopped himself on the head. *Of course! Why didn't I see it?* Then he hugged Lucy again.

"What was I thinking?" he cried. "I...I've got to go see Shana!"

Matt jumped up to leave, then glanced at the clothes scattered on the floor. Lucy winked.

"Don't worry," she said. "I'll take care of this."

"But my uniform is in the washer," Matt said.

Lucy smiled. "I'll take care of that, too. I'll put it in the dryer and fold it for you."

"Thanks!" Matt hugged his sister once again. Then he bolted down the stairs. "And I'm sorry," he called over his shoulder.

Lucy chuckled as she gathered up the towels and placed them on the shelf. *Big brother or not, Matt has a lot to learn about women...*

Shana was trying to study, but she wasn't getting much done. She'd been trying to study all day, but was having trouble concentrating. Mostly because she was feeling bad about the way she treated Matt. Shana knew now that she needed to be honest with him. If she didn't want to do laundry with Matt, then she didn't *have* to—even if that's how every other boyfriend and girlfriend at college did it.

Finally, Shana closed the book and reached for the telephone. She knew she wasn't going to get anything done until she spoke to Matt and settled their problem once and for all.

But just as Shana began to dial, she heard a knock at her door.

"Who is it?" she called, rising.

"It's me," a voice said. "Matt."

Shana pulled the door open and dragged him inside.

"I'm sorry," she said, throwing her arms around him.

"No, *I'm* the one who's sorry," Matt said,

burying his face in her neck. "This whole laundry thing was crazy."

"I'm glad you agree," Shana sighed.

"It was a really stupid idea," said Matt.

Shana sighed and pulled him close. Then she held his head in her hands and looked into his eyes.

"I just think we need more time together before we do laundry."

Then they both giggled.

"I...I talked to your mom today," Shana told him. "She helped me a lot. She's a really great woman. You're lucky to have her."

"I know," Matt said. "Things have been tense at home—with the birth of the twins, my father's heart attack, Mary's basketball insanity, Simon's manic-depressive cycles, and Lucy... being Lucy."

Matt paused. "I don't know how Mom stays so calm and focused, but she does."

"So everything is all right at home?" Shana asked.

"I just want to talk to Mary," Matt said. Then he pulled Shana close again.

"Then maybe we can spend..." He kissed her.

"…some time…" They kissed again.

"…together tomorrow night."

Shana pushed him away with a look of disappointment.

"Oh, Matt," she said with a sigh. "I have to study."

"That's okay," Matt replied. "I just remembered I have to work the dinner shift at the hospital."

"We don't get a break, do we?" Shana said. Then she looked at him and took a deep breath.

"Look, Matt," she began. "Before we run off in separate directions, could I tell you something about me?"

"Sure. Yes. Please."

"When I was growing up, I knew my home life was different from other kids'."

"I know," Matt replied. She touched his lips with her finger.

"Let me say it," she said. Matt nodded.

"I knew I was different, so I tried to make myself fit in by doing well in school, and it worked. I felt good because I was just as smart as all those *normal* kids, and I felt good because all the *normal* kids respected me and paid attention to me."

Shana paused. Matt stood silently, waiting for her to continue.

"Working hard at school made me feel good about myself," she said. "And soon my self-respect was all entwined in grades and academic achievement and, along the way, I really started to enjoy everything about school.

"Now, after all that effort for all those years, after trying to fit into *normal* for so long, I find myself in a position where I might get to pull away from the pack and actually get to go to medical school and become a doctor."

Shana looked into Matt's eyes, searching for understanding.

"That's my dream, Matt," she said. "And you scare me!"

"Me?"

"You scare me because getting *close* to you scares me. I don't want to get sidetracked from my dream."

"Don't worry," Matt said. "I won't get in your way."

"Look," Shana said, hugging him. "I know you've decided you want to be a doctor, too, but it's new for you. You're just starting to invest in that dream, but I've got my whole heart—my whole *life*—tied up in it."

Matt lifted her chin and kissed her.

"Is there room left in there for me?" he asked.

Shana smiled.

"Don't worry," she promised. "I'll make room. But you have to give me time."

"If time is what you need, then time is what you'll get," Matt said.

Shana pointed to her books, still lying in a pile on the couch.

"Now I've got to get going," she said. "I've still got lots of studying to do."

Matt moved to the door. He was almost gone when Shana called to him

"It was nice talking to you," she said.

Matt smiled. "Nice talking to you, too," he replied. "I think we should talk like this more often."

CHAPTER EIGHT

SIMONIZING

"Who is this again?" Mary's voice sounded hollow through the bathroom door.

"You know perfectly well who this is," Matt said, knocking on the door again.

"What are you doing up here?"

"I came up to your room to see you." Matt banged his head against the door. "Now will you come out? Lucy's waiting for you. You have to go to school."

"Tell Lucy to go to school without me."

Matt rolled his eyes. "Look, I'm not your messenger—"

"Stop right there!" Mary cried. "I've heard that argument before. In fact, I *invented* it."

"Fine."

Matt slumped against the door and sank to

the floor. He sighed and looked at Lucy.

Lucy, who had watched the scene with amusement, gathered up the rest of her stuff and headed downstairs to wait for the school bus. She winked and gave Matt a thumbs-up before she slipped away.

"You're going to have to come out sometime," Matt said.

"Actually, I'm not," Mary replied. "I'm thinking of signing up for independent study and finishing the school year in here."

"What can you learn in a bathroom?"

"Plumbing."

"Look," Matt said. "I told you that you were selfish, but I know you're not selfish and I apologize."

There was a long silence. Then he heard the lock click. Still leaning against the door, he struggled to rise. But Mary was faster.

As she burst through the door, Matt lost his balance and plunged headfirst into the bathroom.

"You're right! I have been a little selfish," Mary cried. "Maybe even a *lot* selfish—okay, *completely* selfish—and I was being completely selfish when I told Lucy she was betraying me by going to that party tonight."

Matt, who had finally untangled himself from the shower curtain, stumbled to his feet.

"Okay," he said. "But could we talk about me?"

Mary faced him.

"It's hard to care about your family," Matt told her, "and yet grow up and leave your family—"

"Is that about you?" Mary said. "Because it sounds like it's about me."

"How could it be you?" he replied. "I'm the one who left."

Mary snorted. "And yet you're still here."

"It's comforting to come here, especially when my one relationship outside of here has been..." Matt paused. "Well...a little shaky lately."

"How is it now?" Mary asked, sounding sincere.

"It's good," Matt said. "Really good."

"Then go home!" Mary cried, pointing to her bedroom door. "The bus is coming in ten minutes and I have to talk to my sister before we get to school."

Matt hugged her and took off. He met Lucy

at the door. She ignored him and walked right over to Mary.

"I'm not going," she said.

"No, you *should* go," Mary replied. "You were right. You didn't do anything, and you shouldn't suffer being left out just because I'm ostracized."

Lucy blinked. "*Ostracized*. That's a pretty big word for you."

"Well," Mary said, chuckling, "I've had a lot of time to study. Being left out and all. The library is just about the only place where nobody knows who I am—probably because I've hardly ever *been* there before now."

Lucy looked at Mary, and understood for the first time how bravely her sister was facing her uncertain and clouded future.

"I love you, sis," Lucy said.

Mary hugged her. "I love you, too."

"And if you keep up all this studying," Lucy said, "I'll bet you could be a Rhodes scholar by the end of the year."

Mary scratched her head. "What's that?"

"Never mind. By the end of the year, they'll be letting you back into all the parties."

"Sounds good to me," Mary said doubtfully.

"And I'm still not going to the party tonight."

"Why not?" Mary cried. "Aren't your worried that Tina or Lisa will steal Andrew Nayloss away from you?"

"Nope," Lucy replied. "If they can do that, then he just wasn't the right guy for me anyway."

Mary shook her head. "Luce, you *are* truly amazing."

"Hi, Dad. Bye, Dad."

Matt raced through the kitchen and out the back door. Along the way, he snatched a slice of toast from a plate on the counter.

Reverend Camden looked at his wife. "Does he still live here?"

"Now, now," Mrs. Camden said, wagging her finger. "Matt's had a tough week, but things are better now. I spoke to Shana yesterday. And I just had a talk with him, too. I think things will work out."

"Good," Reverend Camden said, kissing her cheek. "And how goes it with the Master of Disaster, the Grim Reaper of Glenoak, Mr. Doom and Gloom himself—"

"Okay, okay!" she said. "I had a long talk with Simon, too. Let's just say that he's changed the way he looks at the world. And he's helped improve the general mood around here ever since."

Reverend Camden's eyes went skyward. "Thank you," he whispered.

"And you'll be happy to know that Matt and Mary are talking again, and Lucy and Mary are resolving their differences even as we speak. The only dark cloud is that they've missed their bus. I'll have to give Lucy the keys."

"Our youngest officially licensed driver with the keys!" Reverend Camden exclaimed, clutching his chest. "I think I may have another heart attack."

"And," she added, ignoring his theatrics, "you'll be happy to know that the twins have just been changed, so you're spared that little chore."

"You know this can't last," Reverend Camden said. "Something is bound to happen"—he glanced at his watch—"just about any minute."

"*Now* look who's Simonizing," Mrs. Camden replied, handing him a slice of toast.

CHAPTER NINE

KNOCK, KNOCK

Ruthie hopped off the school bus and scurried to the mailbox. Since the twins had arrived, everyone in the Camden family had his or her own special chore. Ruthie's chore was bringing in the mail.

The mailbox was mounted pretty high for a little girl, but Ruthie had a lawn chair close. She slid it under the mailbox and climbed aboard. Fishing around in the box, Ruthie came up empty-handed. She jumped down— and heard a squeak.

"Hello?" she called. She heard another tiny squeak. Then something warm and furry brushed against her leg. Ruthie looked down. A little orange kitten stared up at her and blinked.

"Meow!"

Ruthie took the kitten in her arms and it melted against her, purring happily. The little girl looked toward heaven.

"Thank you for sending me a friend," she said.

"So how was school? And how's Glenoak's newest licensed driver?" Mrs. Camden said.

"Fantastic!" Lucy cried, bubbling with excitement. "I *love* the freedom of driving down the road with the wind in my hair. It's very exhilarating."

Simon rolled his eyes. "You can't feel the wind when you're only going five miles an hour."

Mary winked at her mother. "Simon thinks Lucy drives too slow."

Mrs. Camden leaned close to Mary. "Let me clue you in," she whispered. "When it comes to having your children drive a car, there's no such thing as too slow."

"Thank you, Mom, for defending me," Lucy said. Then she turned to Mary. "And I was only driving slow because you had your big feet hanging out the window."

"Hey," Mary replied, "I had to give my dogs some air."

"From now on, keep your dogs in the car," said Mrs. Camden.

"Dogs!" Simon cried. "Try *horses*."

"Excuse me, *pinhead*!" Mary said, punching him playfully. He ducked her swing, then tried to tickle her. Mary easily held him off.

Lucy and Mrs. Camden exchanged knowing glances. "They've been like this all the way home."

Then Lucy scanned the kitchen. "Did Ruthie get the mail yet?"

"Oops," Mrs. Camden replied. "I already brought it in."

"And?"

Mrs. Camden handed Lucy an envelope.

"Yes!" she cried, jumping up and down. "My official license has arrived!" Lucy already had the paper license from her driver's test, but she was dying to show off the official version— lamination, photo, the works!

She tore open the envelope. "I can't wait to see—"

Lucy's eyes went wide with horror when she saw the image on the license. "That...

that can't be me!" she moaned.

"And yet it is," said Simon with a chuckle. Then Mary burst out laughing.

Mrs. Camden sneaked a peek over Lucy's shoulder and tried not to snicker. Then she heard the door open in the living room.

Saved.

"Someone's at the front door," she said. "I have to go." Mrs. Camden retreated before she lost control.

Mary grinned at Lucy. "Nice picture," she said.

"Don't laugh," Lucy hissed. "You have big feet."

"Yeah," Mary replied. "But I'm not required to carry a picture of them in my wallet."

"You have to smell these," Reverend Camden said, handing his wife a bouquet of roses.

"Oh, Eric!" she cried. "Is this a bribe, or does this mean your checkup went well?"

"My good cholesterol is very good, and my bad cholesterol is very, very good, and my blood pressure is stupendous."

She kissed him. "I'm very proud of you."

He grinned. "I'm proud of myself. I'm really

learning how to deal with stress."

Mrs. Camden led him into the kitchen. She took down a vase, then began to cut and arrange the flowers.

"I've learned how to take stress and use it to help me face whatever challenge life puts in front of me," Reverend Camden said.

"I hope life takes a break from putting challenges in front of you," Mrs. Camden replied. "If the past few months were a test, you passed."

She took the flowers back into the foyer and placed them on a table. Just then, the doorbell rang.

"Don't answer that," Mrs. Camden said.

But Reverend Camden just smiled at her. "I have to. But don't worry. I am calm, I am strong, I am capable of handling any challenge."

He opened the door.

His sister Julie was on the porch, suitcase in hand. The last time Reverend Camden had seen her, she was expecting a baby. Now she was really, really expecting.

"Hi, Julie!" he said, the smile still plastered on his face.

"I'm leaving my husband," Julie said. "We tried to work it out, but it's over!"

Mrs. Camden looked at her husband. He took a deep breath and continued to smile.

"I am calm. I am strong. I am capable of handling any challenge," he said.

"Great!" Julie replied. "Are you capable of carrying my suitcase?"

Julie pushed past him and hugged Mrs. Camden.

"I'm not having a baby with *that man*," she sobbed. "The marriage was a big mistake." Then she looked at Reverend Camden. "A big mistake that's all *your* fault."

"My…me?" Reverend Camden stammered.

"You're my brother, Eric. You know how I am," Julie cried. "If you tell me to go left, I go right. If you hadn't disliked *that man* so much, I never would have married him."

"Go make some tea," Mrs. Camden told her husband.

Simon was waiting for his father in the kitchen.

"Is there going to be dinner tonight?" he asked.

"Of course there's going to be dinner, Simon. We'll just order a couple of pizzas—"

"You can't eat pizza," Simon reminded him. "Cholesterol."

"Then I'll just grab something healthy down at the hospital," Reverend Camden replied. "*After* I have a little chat with my brother-in-law, Hank."

Simon shook his head. "Shouldn't you ask Aunt Julie first? Maybe she doesn't want you to talk to Dr. Hank."

Reverend Camden waved his son off. Then he grabbed his keys and headed out the back door.

As Simon watched his father go, he shook his head. "I'm only thirteen, and even I know that he should ask Aunt Julie first."

Just then, Happy trotted down the back stairs and into the kitchen. She sat down in front of Simon, barked twice, then turned tail and ran back up the stairs.

Curious about Happy's strange behavior, Simon ran up the steps behind the little dog.

"Wait up, Lassie," he called. "Little Timmy is right behind you."

* * *

"I don't smell dinner cooking," Lucy announced. Her grin was sly.

Mary put down her psychology book. "Which means the adults are too busy with Aunt Julie to cook…"

"Which means Mom and Dad might let us go out to eat!"

Mary pointed at her sister. "But *you're* not driving."

Lucy looked crushed.

"Please," Mary continued. "It would be faster to put a saddle on Happy and ride her to dinner than to let you drive. No offense."

Lucy shot her sister a nasty look. "None taken."

The phone rang, and Mary grabbed it. She grinned, covered the receiver, and turned to Lucy.

"It's Andrew Nayloss—for you."

Lucy mouthed a silent scream. Then she regained her composure and took the phone out of Mary's hand.

"Hey, Andrew," she said in a tone she hoped was casual.

Lucy and Andrew talked for a while, and Mary tried to read and not listen in. Finally,

Lucy's eyes went wide and she smiled broadly.

"Sure, I'd love to see a movie tonight!" Lucy winked at Mary.

"Great," Andrew told Lucy. "Pick me up at eight."

Lucy paused. "Pick *you* up?"

"Well," he explained, "I don't have my license yet, and I heard you do, so yeah, you'd have to pick *me* up."

Lucy considered it for a moment. "Fine," she said. "But I'll see you at seven, not eight…okay?"

"Okay," Andrew said. "See you then."

Lucy hung up and looked at Mary. "Andrew asked me out."

"Cool," Mary replied. "But wasn't he going to the big homecoming party tonight—along with everybody else?"

Lucy shook her head. "He told me his dad didn't think that party would be chaperoned properly."

Mary shivered. "Maybe I should come along with you two tonight," she said. "To chaper-one."

Lucy rolled her eyes. "He wants me to drive. Can I do that?"

Mary shrugged. "Sure, but you're not taking the new car."

"Why not?"

"Because I'm taking the new car," Mary said. "Mom and Dad cut me loose and said I could go out tonight—and I intend to travel in style."

"Why can't you travel in style in Dad's minivan?" Lucy demanded.

Mary crossed her arms and shook her head. "No way."

"Mom's new car is a van, too," Lucy countered.

"Yeah," Mary said. "A cool new electric van—big difference!"

"We'll see!" Lucy cried over her shoulder as she bolted from the room and down the stairs. Mary was hot on her heels.

They burst into the living room together. Aunt Julie smiled when she saw them, and they both gave her a hug. Then Lucy cornered her mother.

"Andrew Nayloss asked me out to the movies tonight," she began. "But he doesn't have his license yet, so he asked if I could drive...would that be okay?"

Mrs. Camden stifled a laugh, then nodded. "As long as you're not going too far and you have him home by curfew."

Mary chuckled. Lucy glared at her.

"Do you mind if I take your new car?" Lucy asked.

Mary opened her mouth to protest, but Mrs. Camden was faster.

"Sure," she told Lucy. "Go ahead."

"But I need your new car!" Mary whined.

"To go where?" Mrs. Camden asked, her eyebrow raised.

Mary blinked. "Well...I don't *know* yet."

"Well, you can't just go out driving around," Mrs. Camden told her. "You have to have a plan."

"Yeah," said Lucy.

"Okay," Mary said after thinking it over. "I could take the kids out and feed them dinner so you guys could have the house to yourselves."

Mrs. Camden smiled. "That would be great. Just grab some cash out of the coffee can."

Mary nodded. "So that means *I* can have the car?"

"Yes," Mrs. Camden replied. "Your father's minivan."

Lucy smiled in triumph and marched out of the living room. Mary followed her, a sour look on her face.

"Eric was supposed to be making tea, wasn't he?" Aunt Julie asked.

Mrs. Camden nodded.

"That's just like men! Can't depend on them for anything."

Mrs. Camden jumped to her feet. "Do you want some tea?" she asked.

Aunt Julie shook her head. "No. Of course not."

CHAPTER TEN

LUCY'S NIGHT OUT

Mary and Lucy found Simon on the stairs.

"Get ready," Mary said. "I'm taking you and Ruthie out for dinner."

"Cool. But what about Lucy?" Simon asked.

Mary made a face. "She's taking a guy out on a date."

"In Mom's new car," Lucy added.

Simon patted Lucy on the back. "Wow. That's very emancipated of you," he said. "Asking a guy out is tough."

Lucy rolled her eyes. "I didn't...he...never mind."

With a wave of her hand, Lucy went to her room to prepare for her big date with Andrew Nayloss.

"If Lucy's driving Mom's car, how are we going to go out?" Simon asked.

Mary frowned. "We've got Dad's minivan."

"No, we don't. Dad *took* the minivan."

"What?"

"Yeah," Simon said with a nod. "He went to the hospital to talk to Uncle Hank about Aunt Julie."

Mary shook her head. "What was he thinking? Dad is so wrong."

"I know, I know," Simon replied. "I tried to tell him."

Mary turned on her heels and headed back to the living room.

Before Simon followed his sister, he took another look at Happy, who sat expectantly in front of the twins' bedroom door. No matter what Simon did to entice the dog, Happy refused to budge.

An equally stubborn Ruthie refused to let the dog into the twins' bedroom, where she claimed she was baby-sitting.

Simon knew something was definitely up.

Mrs. Camden and Aunt Julie stopped talking when Mary returned to the living room.

"What's wrong?"

"Dad took the minivan," Mary said, trying not to look at Aunt Julie.

"Really," Mrs. Camden said. "That's odd. He just up and left without telling me?"

You don't want to go there, Mom. Mary cleared her throat. "I...I think he went to, ah...*visit* someone..."

Mrs. Camden missed Mary's cues, but Aunt Julie didn't.

"Oh, no," she groaned, clutching her tummy. "He didn't go to see Hank, did he? Eric better *not* have!"

Mrs. Camden looked shocked. Mary looked away. And Aunt Julie looked as if she was ready to explode—in more ways than one!

"Ow!" Aunt Julie cried. "I'm having a cramp."

Reverend Camden scanned the array of cafeteria food spread out before him with a wary eye. He wasn't quite sure what was less appealing—the food or the hair net his son Matt was wearing as he dished up servings for his customers.

"Okay, Dad, here's the menu." Matt rubbed his hands together. "We have your fried slop..."

He pointed to a greasy mess of meat in a large aluminum tray. "And here's your sautéed slop. And here"—he dipped a large metal spoon into a tray full of unidentifiable mush—"is your really old orange slop."

Matt lifted a finger. "I have to warn you," he said, "I hear the orange slop is a little spicy."

Reverend Camden made a face. "I think I'll just have some Jell-O."

Matt leaned over the glass counter. "Take one from the back. They make us shove the really old ones to the front."

Reverend Camden felt a little queasy.

"So, Dad," Matt said, "why are you risking your good health by eating hospital food?"

"I'm waiting to talk to your Uncle Hank about your Aunt Julie," he replied. "But I'm told he's in the middle of a delivery."

"What's wrong with Aunt Julie?" Matt asked. He had always liked his father's free-spirited sister.

"Sadly, she's over at our house, perhaps permanently."

"Huh?"

"It seems Uncle Hank isn't treating her very well."

Matt shook his head doubtfully. "And you just felt it was your duty to run to the hospital and tell him?"

"Yes," Reverend Camden said, somewhat defensively. "Julie's my sister. I care if she's not happy."

"So Hank is wrong and you're right," Matt said.

"Correct," said Reverend Camden with a nod.

Matt smiled. "And this has nothing to do with Hank one-upping you when he saved your life after the heart attack?"

Reverend Camden frowned. "Just give me my Jell-O."

Mrs. Camden hung up the phone and turned back to Mary and Aunt Julie.

"They can't find Hank," Mrs. Camden explained. "He might be in surgery."

"Hank is never around when I need him," Aunt Julie cried. "My marriage is a sham!"

Mrs. Camden reached for the phone again. "We'll page him."

But Aunt Julie shook her head. "It won't do any good," she sobbed. "He's probably out with one of his patient friends. Do you know that one of his patients is a supermodel?"

"Really?" Mary said excitedly.

Mrs. Camden dug her elbow into Mary's ribs, silencing her.

"Oh, yes," Aunt Julie continued. "Being a model wasn't good enough for *her*. *She* had to be a *super* model!"

Aunt Julie reached into her pocket.

"Here," she said, tossing Mary the keys. "Take my car. I'm not going anywhere."

Then Aunt Julie broke down in tears. As Mrs. Camden reached out to comfort her, she shot Mary a look that said "Get lost."

She didn't have to ask twice.

Mary banged on the bedroom door, causing Happy to jump to her feet and bark excitedly.

"Come on, Ruthie, we're going to dinner."

"I don't want to go," Ruthie called through the door.

Simon looked at Mary, then down at Happy. His eyebrow lifted suspiciously.

"Why don't you want to go?" Mary called.

The door flew open a crack, and Ruthie

slipped out, careful not to let the dog into the room behind her.

"I want to stay home and look after the twins," Ruthie lied.

Simon and Mary exchanged glances, then Mary shrugged. "Okay," she said. "Suit your-self."

When they were gone, Ruthie went back into the room. The twins were snoozing in the playpen, but Ruthie ignored them. She ran to a pile of cushions and pulled down the baby blanket she'd tossed there.

"They're all gone," she whispered to the sleeping kitten. "It's just you and me, my little friend…"

Out in the hallway, Happy whimpered and pawed at the door.

Lucy's heart was fluttering with excitement as she passed the park and pulled up to the big house that belonged to the Nayloss family. Unlike the Camdens' quaint old Victorian, the Nayloss family's home was ultramodern, with a huge Japanese garden and a long stone path leading up to the front door. Lucy felt almost intimidated until she glanced at her reflection in the rearview mirror.

She had decided to wear her new black slacks and matching turtleneck sweater. Over everything she wore a fashionable Ralph Lauren black leather jacket—a reward to herself for working all summer. Lucy felt confident and sophisticated as she parked the van and climbed out.

An attractive middle-aged woman in a long dress was waiting for Lucy on the front porch. She smiled as Lucy approached.

"Hi. I'm Lucy Camden...Andrew's date."

The woman turned. "I'll go get Andrew," she said. As Mrs. Nayloss vanished through the front door, Mr. Nayloss came out and walked up to Lucy. He had a scowl on his face.

"Where are you going tonight?" he barked. His tone made Lucy jump.

"Ah...the movies," she said. The man glowered at her.

"Andrew asked *me* out," Lucy added. "I'm...I'm just driving."

"And how long have you been driving?" Mr. Nayloss demanded.

"A few weeks. I got my permanent license

today," Lucy replied, hoping he wouldn't ask to see it.

"Then you better stay off busy streets, and you better have Andrew home by ten sharp!"

"Okay!" Lucy said, nodding quickly.

"I know how you girls are." Mr. Nayloss mumbled.

"What?" Lucy said.

Mr. Nayloss stared at her. "Have you ever been arrested?" he demanded.

"Huh?"

"You heard me." Mr. Nayloss studied her as if she was a suspect standing in a police lineup.

"Hey, Lucy," Andrew called from the front door. Lucy breathed a sigh of relief.

"Have fun, you two," Mrs. Nayloss called from the house.

As Andrew crossed the sidewalk toward her, Mr. Nayloss leaned close to Lucy and whispered in her ear.

"Ten o'clock," he growled. "Not a minute later or I call the police."

Then the man stood up and turned to his son. Suddenly, he was wearing a big smile. "Have a good time, Andrew," he said.

As Mr. Nayloss went inside, Andrew crossed

to the passenger side of the car. He stood at the door for a moment. Lucy, confused, waited for him to climb inside.

"That's okay," Andrew said at last. "I can get my own door."

Lucy blinked. *Did he expect me to open the door for him?*

Reverend Camden was sitting at a table with Matt, finishing his "meal," when Hank—still wearing surgical scrubs—burst into the cafeteria.

"So you got me out of a difficult labor to watch you eat Jell-O?" he said, throwing up his hands. "That's just fantastic, Eric. It's been fun, but I've got to get back to my delivery."

Hank turned to leave.

"Your wife left you," Reverend Camden said.

Hank froze. "What did you say?"

"Julie left you." Reverend Camden motioned Hank to a chair.

"This is about the supermodel, isn't it?" Hank said, shaking his head and plopping down in the chair.

"You're seeing a supermodel?" Matt said, impressed.

"She's a patient," Hank replied, bopping Matt on the forehead. "Supermodels go through difficult pregnancies, too."

"Is your supermodel having a scheduled birth?" Matt asked. Reverend Camden and Hank gave him a puzzled look.

"Well," Matt explained, "I...I might be working that day."

"Check with my office," Hank said, rolling his eyes.

"Really?"

"No!" Hank said, bopping Matt's head again.

"So what are you going to do about Julie?" Reverend Camden asked.

Hank sighed. "She knew what I did for a living before she married me. I'm always going to have female patients. Eventually, she'll calm down, and I promise to call her as soon as I get two seconds."

Hank rose. "But right now, I've got to get back into the delivery room."

"A supermodel," Matt gushed. "Wow!"

Reverend Camden reached over and bopped his son on the head. Then he jumped up and followed Hank out of the cafeteria.

"That's it?" Reverend Camden cried. "That's the best you can do?"

"Look," Hank said, "you don't know what I've been going through. Julie has been a complete basket case, and no matter how much I love her, she is going to have to control her insanity. I can't take it anymore. Do you have any idea what it's like living with someone who is irrational and insane twenty-four hours a day?"

Reverend Camden gave him a smug smile. "Yes, I do," he replied. "I've experienced it, let's see...six wonderful times now. But I think the bigger issue is that you have never had to live with it once."

Hank rolled his eyes again. "I've spent my entire career around pregnant women," he said.

"Yes," Reverend Camden replied. "But not the *same* pregnant woman—and never your pregnant *wife*."

Hank knew that his brother-in-law had gotten him, and he didn't like it. Not one little bit.

"You don't know what you're talking about," Hank said, storming off to the delivery room.

Matt looked at his father. "So what are you going to do now? Are you going home?"

"I'm not going anywhere," Reverend Camden said. "I just found Dr. Hank Hastings's Achilles' heel."

Matt looked stricken. "It's not the super-model, is it?"

CHAPTER ELEVEN

MAKING FRIENDS

Lucy and Andrew were enjoying their date. They stood in line, waiting to get into the movie, and talked about the big homecoming party for the boys' basketball team.

"So why didn't you go?" Andrew asked.

"I didn't feel right about it," Lucy said. "Not after the way everyone's been treating Mary."

"My father was upset when he heard I was going out with a Camden girl," Andrew told her. "But I told him you weren't the one who trashed the gym—you were her sister."

"Uh...thanks," Lucy replied. *How embarrassing!* But at least she knew where Mr. Nayloss's comment about getting arrested had come from!

There was a pause as they stepped up to the cashier's window. The pause continued for a long, awkward minute. Lucy glanced at Andrew, who waited expectantly.

"The suspense is killing me," the cashier said.

Lucy smiled and said, "Two students, please."

The cashier nodded. Lucy looked at Andrew hopefully, but he didn't make a move for his wallet. Reluctantly, Lucy reached into her purse and drew out a twenty. Andrew smiled.

"I'll get the popcorn," he offered.

"Great," said Lucy.

Andrew opened the door and walked into the theater. The door swung closed in Lucy's face. *How rude!*

Lucy made a face and pushed through. *Oh, this is fun*, she thought sourly.

Mary ended up taking Simon to the pool hall for dinner. The burgers were good, but they were both disappointed to find that the place was mostly deserted. Everyone was at the big homecoming party.

"So," Mary said as they finished their meal,

"it's Friday night. How come you and Deena don't have a date?"

"We're only allowed to go out together one night a week," Simon explained.

Mary raised her eyebrow. "Since when?"

"Since her father caught us kissing in her den." Simon actually blushed.

Mary's jaw dropped. "This is new."

"I'm surprised Deena's dad reacted the way he did," Simon continued. "Deena and I discussed our kissing options and we both thought that if we got caught, since her dad isn't a minister he would be—shall we say— more liberal?"

He shook his head sadly. "We were wrong."

While Simon sopped up his ketchup with the few remaining fries, Mary noticed a freshman from Glenoak watching them. Mary studied the cute blonde. She was definitely watching them. As Simon drained his glass, the girl got up and approached their table.

"Aren't you Mary Camden," she said, "the basketball player?"

Mary smiled brightly. "Yes."

"Wow! I've seen you play." She stuck out her hand. "Hi, I'm Diane Hardt."

Then the girl turned to Simon. "Please tell me this isn't your date."

Mary laughed. Simon extended his hand. "I'm not her date," he said. "I'm her brother, Simon."

Diane took his hand, and her touch lingered. "I'm glad to hear that," she said.

"My *thirteen-year-old* brother," Mary added pointedly.

Diane ignored her. "Would you like to join us?" Simon asked.

"That'd be great," Diane replied. She pulled a chair close to Simon and sat down.

"So," Mary purred, "how old are you, Diane?"

"Fifteen," she said, turning to Simon and touching his hand. "But I'm a *young* fifteen."

Mrs. Camden watched Aunt Julie pace—more like waddle—across the living room floor.

"What's the problem?" she asked. "Are you in pain?"

"I'll tell you what the problem is," Aunt Julie began. "The problem is that Hank and I aren't ready to be parents."

Mrs. Camden waved her hand. "That's silly.

You and Hank are going to be wonderful parents."

Aunt Julie snorted. "Here's a big slice of irony for you," she cried. "I'm making bad decisions sober. Sober! Can you believe that? At least when I drank, I didn't go out and do something stupid like get married!"

She plopped down on the sofa. "My back is killing me," she said.

Mrs. Camden jumped to her feet. "I'll go get a hot-water bottle. That will make you feel better."

The hospital cafeteria was closed for the evening. Most of the chairs were up on tables, and Matt was busy with a bucket and mop, cleaning the floor.

Sitting at a corner table, Reverend Camden read a newspaper and sipped a cup of lukewarm tea.

Just as Matt finished mopping and placed the SLIPPERY WHEN WET sign at the entrance, Hank burst through the door, still wearing his surgical scrubs.

Matt smiled. "Hey, Uncle Hank. How did the delivery go?"

Hank walked up to Reverend Camden and looked down at him.

"Twins," he said without turning to Matt. "A boy and a girl, six pounds each. Mother and babies are doing fine."

Reverend Camden set his paper down and looked up at Hank, who stared at him.

"So let me get this straight," Hank said, wagging his finger at Reverend Camden. "What you're saying is—"

"That no matter how many pregnant women you've been around, you still don't know how to cope with your own pregnant wife," Reverend Camden said smugly.

"Well," Hank cried, "I think you're...I think you're..." Dejectedly, he plopped down on a chair next to Reverend Camden. "I think you are absolutely correct."

Hank buried his face in his hands. "The last couple of months have been unbearable," he moaned. "No matter what I do, it's wrong. No matter what I say, it's wrong. I'm at the end of my rope."

Reverend Camden patted his shoulder. "Get cleaned up," he said. "I'll take you out to dinner and we can talk."

"Thanks," Hank said.

"So where are we going?" Matt asked. Reverend Camden and Hank exchanged glances.

"Come on, you guys," Matt begged. "You can't just leave me here all by myself on a Friday night."

"Hey, I've got an idea," Hank said after a pause. "Why doesn't Matt join us?"

Reverend Camden shook his head. "Now why didn't I think of that?"

"Great!" Matt cried, racing to the back of the cafeteria. "Just let me get cleaned up."

"This is a kitty," Ruthie said, holding up the struggling cat to show the twins. Sam and David rolled around in their playpen. But when they saw the kitten, they both cooed with delight.

"Can you say 'Hello, Kitty'?"

Sam reached out to touch the kitten. David rolled over and crawled under his blanket.

"Say 'Hello, Kitty,'" Ruthie insisted.

David poked his head out from under the baby blanket and made an unintelligible sound.

"See!" Ruthie cried. "I told you kitties are fun."

At that moment, Mrs. Camden came up the steps looking for the hot-water bottle. She recalled she'd left it with the twins. When she got to the bedroom door, she found Happy blocking it. The dog got up and wagged her tail excitedly.

But when Mrs. Camden turned the knob, she discovered the door was locked.

"Oh, Ruthie," Mrs. Camden called. "Why is the door closed?"

"No reason," Ruthie lied. She stuffed the confused kitten into her backpack until only a swishing orange tail stuck out. Then she crossed the room and opened the door.

"Why didn't you go out with Simon and Mary?" Mrs. Camden asked.

"No reason," Ruthie replied.

Mrs. Camden stared at her doubtfully. "What did you have for dinner, then?"

"No reason...er...I mean, a peanut butter and jelly sandwich."

Mrs. Camden gave Ruthie a look filled with suspicion. Then she popped her head through the door and scanned the bedroom.

Everything seemed normal.

As she entered the room, Happy scurried in behind her. Mrs. Camden spotted the hot-water bottle and snatched it from the dresser. Happy plopped down in front of Ruthie's backpack and whimpered.

"I'm going to take Aunt Julie this hot-water bottle," Mrs. Camden said. "And then I'll be back up here to get the twins ready for bed."

"I can give them their bottles," Ruthie said with a smile.

"That's very sweet," Mrs. Camden replied. "But I still think you're up to something."

Ruthie shrugged.

"I'll be right back," Mrs. Camden warned her.

Just then, they both heard Aunt Julie's frantic cries from the living room. "Annie!" she called. "I need a little help. Hurry!"

Mrs. Camden rushed down the stairs. Ruthie turned to grab her backpack, but saw Happy guarding it.

"Shoo!" Ruthie cried, chasing the dog away from the kitten.

Mrs. Camden was halfway down the stairs when she saw Ruthie eject Happy from the bedroom. Her eyes narrowed.

Ruthie was definitely up to something!

Moments later, Mrs. Camden rushed to Julie's side, a full hot-water bottle in hand.

"I'm...I'm not feeling so good," Julie moaned. She didn't look too good, either.

"What's wrong?" Mrs. Camden asked, still clutching the hot-water bottle.

"I don't really know. I have this cramping thing going on," Julie said. "Maybe it's an upset stomach or something. I haven't eaten much today—owwww!"

Julie tried to stand, but Mrs. Camden pushed her back down onto the couch. She tucked some pillows behind her.

"You have cramps and your back hurts?" Mrs. Camden asked nervously.

Julie nodded. "Yeah," she said, puzzled. "All of a sudden my back is killing me. Do you think it's something I ate?"

Mrs. Camden made a face. "It's not some-thing you ate," she said. "But it might be some-thing you are about to have."

Julie's eyes went wide. "Oh, no, don't say that I'm about to give—owwww!" The pain was so sharp that she almost bent double.

Mrs. Camden nodded. "I think you may be in labor."

"That's impossible," Julie cried. "I'm only eight months pregnant."

You have a lot to learn, kiddo, Mrs. Camden thought.

"Besides," Julie gasped, the pain subsiding, "I can't be in labor because I'm not going to have a baby with *that man*."

Suddenly, Julie began to cry. "I'm going to have a baby, aren't I?"

"Don't worry," Mrs. Camden said, placing pillows around her. "Everything is going to be just fine. I'll make you comfortable until... someone gets back."

Julie's tears continued to flow. Mrs. Camden sat down on the couch next to the distraught woman and cradled her in her arms.

"Everything is going to be fine...," she said. But the look of concern on Mrs. Camden's face told a very different story.

Where is Mary? Where is Lucy? Where is Matt? And where are our husbands?

CHAPTER TWELVE

BUSTED

Mrs. Camden didn't want to panic—not in front of Julie. So she put on a happy face, despite the fact that Julie's pains were becoming worse, and nobody had yet returned— which meant no car, and no way to get to the hospital.

A lull in Julie's pains gave Mrs. Camden the chance to go to the kitchen. There she spied her husband's beeper on the counter. He had forgotten to take it when he had vanished earlier that evening.

Mrs. Camden decided it was time for action. She peeked in on Julie, who was resting quietly. Then she rushed back to the kitchen and grabbed the phone.

It was time to page both their husbands.

* * *

The "discussion" about where to have dinner continued through the halls of Glenoak Hospital and into the parking lot. Matt didn't care one way or another—he just wanted to eat something besides hospital food. But his father and Uncle Hank couldn't seem to agree on anything, including what type of cuisine they wanted.

Matt knew better than to speak up, but he felt he had to make an effort to break the deadlock between his uncle and his father.

"How about the pool hall?" he said.

"Pool hall?" Reverend Camden groaned.

Uncle Hank shuddered. "Greasy burgers and fries."

Well, Matt thought, *at least they agreed on something*.

"We could go to Mazzio's," Reverend Camden suggested. "It's fine Italian food at a reasonable price."

But Uncle Hank shook his head. "Allergic to tomato sauce."

They argued for a few more minutes, until they had discussed—and rejected—virtually every restaurant within a fifty-mile radius.

Finally, Matt spoke up.

"If you two don't pick a restaurant in the next sixty seconds"—he glanced at his watch—"we're going back inside and it's spicy orange slop for everyone!"

Reverend Camden made a face. "You're the one having a bad night," he said to Hank. "Why don't you pick?"

"I don't think I like your smug tone," Uncle Hank joked.

"I'm not being smug," Reverend Camden said smugly.

Matt held up the watch. "Tick-tock-tick…"

"I know a good health-food restaurant across town," Hank said. Reverend Camden thought about it, then nodded.

"Perfect," Matt said, "now let's go!"

Hank paused. "Maybe I should call Julie…"

But Reverend Camden shook his head. "Trust me. I've seen my sister like this before. Just let her and Annie talk for a little while. We'll call them *after* dinner."

"Okay," Hank replied as Matt pushed them both to their cars.

As they drove away a moment later, the loudspeaker in the parking lot crackled to life.

"Paging Dr. Hastings...paging Reverend Camden...paging Dr. Hastings...This is an emergency..."

"Yes, I understand," Mrs. Camden said into the phone. "But this really is an emergency. Can you continue to page them both, please?"

She hung up the phone. *Where could they be?* she wondered.

Then Mrs. Camden took a deep breath. She was all smiles as she went back out to the living room to break the news to Julie.

"Well, Eric forgot his beeper," Mrs. Camden said. "So I...I can't page him directly."

Julie rolled her eyes. "What about the hospital?"

Mrs. Camden sat down. "I'm having them both paged, but so far, nothing. But I did leave a message on your home machine and on Hank's service. I even left a message on Matt's machine—he works at the hospital, and he might have seen them."

Julie stared off into space.

"Feeling better?" Mrs. Camden asked.

Julie shrugged. "That depends," she said. "Does the pain get better or worse?"

Mrs. Camden gave her a look that was full of sympathy. Julie frowned.

"That's what I thought," she moaned.

"But the good news is that if you are in labor and you're having contractions, they are still far enough apart that we can wait a little while longer before we have to get you to the hospital.

"Which brings up the question of how we're going to get to the hospital—we have no car."

Julie paled.

"But don't worry," Mrs. Camden insisted. "If it gets bad, I'll call an ambulance."

"I'm not worried about the labor," Julie said. "I'm worried about going to the hospital and having everyone find out I don't know where my husband is…"

She began to cry again, and Mrs. Camden sat next to her. "A little embarrassment might be okay," she said. "Considering the circumstances."

Julie moaned as another contraction hit her.

"I know where Hank is," she cried. "He's with his supermodel."

Mrs. Camden chuckled. "He's with Eric."

"So? Supermodels have supermodel friends."

Just then, another contraction made Julie moan again.

"That's it," Mrs. Camden declared. "As soon as Mary and Simon come home, we're going to the hospital!"

"And pretty soon I noticed that everyone in the house was in a bad mood," Simon said. "The blues spread like it was contagious or something. So I decided to break the cycle and fix the mess!"

"What did you do?" Diane Hardt asked, hanging on his every word.

"I decided it was time to spread a little cheer," Simon explained. "I discovered that if you act happy, you feel happy. So I acted happy, and pretty soon everyone was happy."

Mary, sitting across from them, stifled a yawn and scanned the pool hall.

"I don't like to brag," Simon concluded, sitting back in his chair. "But it really was my quick thinking that saved the day."

Mary rolled her eyes.

Diane sighed. "Wow..."

"Yeah. Wow," Mary said.

Diane rose. "I'll be right back," she told Simon, and exited toward the bathroom.

Mary looked at Simon. "What are you doing?" she hissed. "I feel like I'm chaperoning a *date* here. That's what mothers are for—not big sisters."

"Don't be ridiculous," Simon scoffed. "Diane is fifteen. She's not interested in me."

"Are you blind as well as boring?"

"Shhh," Simon said. "She's coming back."

"Do you want to play a game of pool?" Diane purred, taking Simon's arm.

"We really should get going," Mary said.

But Simon waved her off. "We have time for a quick game," he said, leaving with Diane.

Mary sighed and sat back in her chair. She watched them as Simon set up the balls and handed Diane a pool cue.

"Oh, Simon?" she cooed. "Am I holding this stick thingy right?"

"Well, let's see," Simon said, standing behind her. Diane bent low and Simon took her arms in his.

"You line it up like this…," he explained.

It was exactly the *wrong* moment for Deena

and her father to walk into the pool hall.

"Simon?" Deena said, her eyes wide.

Simon looked up. Deena was staring at him in disbelief. Mr. Stewart, her father, glared at Simon. Diane smiled coolly.

"Oh, hi!" Simon cried, jumping backward. To cover his embarrassment, he quickly introduced everyone.

"Deena," he began. "this is my girlfriend, Diane...I...I mean *Diane*, this is my girlfriend, *Deena*!"

Mr. Stewart shook his head. Deena looked as if she was about to cry. Mary turned away.

It was just too horrible to watch.

To make matters worse, Diane looked right at Deena. "Why, Simon," she said, "I didn't realize you had a *girlfriend*."

Deena stared at Simon, her lips trembling.

"I'll just give Mary my phone number, in case you ever want to call," Diane said, brushing his face with her hand before slipping away.

CHAPTER THIRTEEN

EMERGENCY

"We need to talk," Ruthie said to Aunt Julie. They were alone. Mrs. Camden was off refilling the hot-water bottle.

"What do we need to talk about?" Aunt Julie asked.

"I heard you yelling," Ruthie said. "Are you having a baby?"

"Maybe," Aunt Julie replied.

"Excellent!" Ruthie said. She reached into her backpack and pulled out the mewing orange kitten.

"Ohhh, how cute," Aunt Julie gushed. "I didn't know you had a cat."

"No one knows," Ruthie whispered. "And no one can know. That's where you come in."

"Me?"

Ruthie nodded. "When you scream, if you yell *me-ouch* instead of *ouch*, whenever my kitten meows, everyone will think it's you. Let's practice."

Aunt Julie said, "Me-ouch," trying not to giggle despite her pain.

"That was good," Ruthie said. "But could you put more cat into it?"

"I'll try."

The little orange cat meowed.

"See," Ruthie said. "Just like that."

"Nothing was going on," Simon told Deena. "Honest!" They sat at their own table, away from Mr. Stewart and Mary, trying to work out their differences. Deena was willing to listen to Simon's explanation, but she still couldn't get the sight of Simon and Diane Hardt together at the pool table out of her head.

"If nothing was going on, why do you look so guilty?" Deena cried. "And why do you keep apologizing?"

Simon shrugged. He didn't know what to say.

"As if being caught making out wasn't bad enough," Deena continued. "Now, because of that girl, my father thinks you're some sort of middle-school Romeo."

"He does?" Simon said, impressed.

Deena shot him an angry look.

"Er…he does?" Simon said, more contritely.

Just then, Mary appeared at Simon's shoulder. "We've got to go home right now," she told him.

"What's wrong?" Simon asked, not happy about leaving Deena.

"Mom paged me here, and the waitress just told me," Mary said breathlessly. "Aunt Julie is in labor…she's going to have her baby!"

Simon jumped up. "Shouldn't she be in a hospital?"

"How do you want them to get there?" Mary replied. "On a go-cart? Lucy has one car, Dad has the other, and we're driving Aunt Julie's."

"We're on our way," Simon said. He looked at Deena, who nodded her understanding.

"I'll call you…," Simon said over his shoulder as Mary dragged him out of the restaurant.

At ten o'clock sharp, Lucy parked the car in front of Andrew Nayloss's house. When she cut the engine, he sat there looking at her expectantly.

"Why not!" Lucy muttered to herself. Then she got out, circled the car, and opened the passenger-side door for him.

"Thanks," Andrew said, climbing out. He stood there, waiting. Lucy gave him a puzzled look.

"Aren't you going to walk me to the door?" Andrew said.

"Sure," Lucy replied, unable to hide her disgust. At the porch, Andrew waited for Lucy to kiss him.

This date could not get any worse, Lucy told herself.

"Well," Andrew said, "I had a great time."

"I know," Lucy replied. "Well, good night."

Just then, Andrew grabbed Lucy and pulled her to him. Before she could react, he landed a big, passionate kiss on her unsuspecting lips.

Then the front door opened and Mr. Nayloss appeared. They broke their kiss immediately. Angrily, Mr. Nayloss glanced at his watch, then glared at Lucy.

"You're late," he declared.

Yeah, Lucy thought. *By about a minute*. But she kept her mouth shut.

"So," Andrew said, "are you free next Friday?"

Lucy looked at Andrew, then at Mr. Nayloss.

"Nah," she said, shaking her head. She practically ran to the minivan and drove away so fast she really *could* feel the wind in her hair. Although she had to admit, the kiss *was* really good.

Mary and Simon burst through the front door and rushed into the living room.

"Mom! Aunt Julie!" Mary cried. Mrs. Camden rushed up to them.

"Is everything okay?" Simon asked.

Mrs. Camden breathed a sigh of relief. "Now it is," she said, taking the car keys from Mary. "Aunt Julie is lying down, resting. But the contractions are coming pretty close together now. I hope it's not too late…"

"What are you going to do?" Simon asked.

"I'm going to take your Aunt Julie to the hospital," Mrs. Camden told him.

"What can *we* do?" Mary asked.

"Stay here and keep an eye on things," her mother said. "Lucy's not home from her date yet, but Sam and David are asleep. And Ruthie…well, Ruthie is up to something. But I'm not sure what."

"Don't worry," Mary said. "I'm here."

"Great," Mrs. Camden cried, hurrying toward the front door.

"Mom?" Mary called.

Mrs. Camden spun around. "What?"

"You forgot Aunt Julie."

Mrs. Camden blinked, then shook her head. "Six pregnancies and I've never been on this side of things before. It's…different."

Just then, Aunt Julie stumbled into the room. She was clutching her back with one hand and her tummy with the other. Mrs. Camden rushed to her side.

"Don't worry," she said. "I've got a car and I'm going to get you to the hospital. Everything is going to be fine."

"I…I think it might be too late," Aunt Julie moaned. "I think I'm about to have my baby…"

CHAPTER FOURTEEN
NEW ARRIVAL

Ruthie crept into the darkened kitchen and grabbed a bowl from the shelf. Then she went to the refrigerator and got the milk. Carefully, she poured a little milk into the bottom of the bowl.

Just then, Lucy came through the back door. "Mary left the car half in the middle of the street," she said. "What's going on around here?"

Ruthie set the milk down and lifted the bowl. "Aunt Julie is having her baby."

Lucy's jaw dropped.

Then Simon came in and turned on the light. "Ruthie's right," he said. "Upstairs, in Mom and Dad's room."

"Unbelievable."

Mary came in and sat down at the table. Simon joined her. Lucy sat down, too. They all noticed Ruthie's bowl.

"Would you like a little cereal with that?" Simon asked.

"Why?" Ruthie said innocently. "I like my milk in a bowl." She got up and walked to the door.

"Where are you going?" Mary asked.

"I...I think I'll enjoy my milk in my room," Ruthie said over her shoulder.

Mary looked at Simon and they both nodded. *She's up to something.*

Then Simon sighed. "I'd better call Deena."

When Simon was gone, Mary twiddled her thumbs for a minute, watching Lucy. "So how was your date?" she asked finally.

Lucy pretended to gag. "Listen to *this*..."

Mrs. Camden plopped the pillows under Julie. She was in a sitting position, and between contractions.

"Where's Hank?" Julie cried. "Didn't you tell me he was coming?"

"The hospital finally reached them at a restaurant. They should be here any minute."

"I'm scared," Julie said.

"I know," Mrs. Camden replied. "But the ambulance is on the way."

"The baby's early. What if something's wrong?" Julie voice was tense with worry.

"A lot of first babies come early," Mrs. Camden.

They both heard heavy steps on the stairs. Seconds later, Hank and Reverend Camden burst into the room.

"We're here! We're here!" Hank cried. He clutched his medical bag.

"Get out!" Julie cried. "Get out!"

Reverend Camden froze in his tracks and turned to flee.

"Not *you*!" Julie cried, pointing to her husband. "*Him*! Get *that man* out of here!"

"Sorry," Reverend Camden said. "He's the only physician on the premises."

"Where have you been all night?" Julie demanded.

Hank stammered an explanation, but Julie waved him off. Then she howled as a contraction hit her.

Mrs. Camden grabbed her husband's arm. "We'll be right outside if you need us," she said, pushing Reverend Camden into the hall.

"I'm scared," Julie said when she was alone with her husband.

"Don't be," he told her. "I love you more than life itself, I will never leave you, and we are going to make fabulous parents...and, by the way, you have never looked more beautiful."

Julie snorted. Then she smiled.

"Now take a deep breath and push...," Hank said, opening his medical bag.

Arm in arm, Reverend Camden and his wife walked down the stairs. When they got to the bottom, the doorbell rang.

"That's probably the ambulance," Mrs. Camden said, kissing her husband's cheek.

But when she opened the door, their new neighbor, Jill Tierney, was standing on the doorstep with her young son.

"Hi, Annie. Eric," she said. "I wouldn't have bothered you so late but I saw the lights were on and..."

"Come in, come in," Mrs. Camden said. "Is there something wrong?"

"Yes," said Mrs. Tierney. "Yes, there is. My

son Billy lost his kitten and, well, we were hoping that maybe you found it. Someone said they saw your daughter with a cat."

"Say no more," Mrs. Camden said. Then she called for Ruthie.

"Yes?" the little girl cried from the top of the stairs.

"Could you come down here, please."

Ruthie marched slowly down the stairs, her backpack slung over her shoulder. Happy was close on her heels, sniffing at the pack.

Mrs. Camden took Ruthie aside. "That little boy lost his kitten," she said.

Billy Tierney walked over to Ruthie and handed her a photo of a tiny orange cat.

"That's sad," Ruthie said, handing the picture back to the little boy.

"Do you know anything about it?" Mrs. Camden asked. Ruthie blinked. Just then, they all heard a loud squeak from inside the backpack.

"That was Aunt Julie!" Ruthie cried.

But at that moment, the kitten struggled out of the backpack and scrambled into Billy's arms.

"Norton!" the boy cried, cradling his cat.

The cat melted against the boy, purring madly. "Oh, Norton! I'm so glad to see you."

Reverend Camden blinked. "Norton?"

Jill Tierney chuckled. *"The Honeymooners,"* she explained.

They watched the boy's reunion with his kitten for a moment. Then Mrs. Tierney spoke. "I don't know how to thank you. We were so worried."

"Just be more careful next time," Ruthie said to Billy. Then she frowned. "That's my baby they're taking away."

"We posted a reward," Mrs. Tierney said, handing Ruthie a twenty-dollar bill. "I hope this will help ease your loss."

Ruthie smiled as she took the money. "It helps, it helps."

"That's too much," Reverend Camden said. But Mrs. Tierney shook her head.

"I insist. We would have paid anything to get Norton back for Billy. Thanks again."

After Lucy told her sister the horrendous story of her date, Mary sighed.

"I guess you wish you'd gone to the homecoming party," she said.

But Lucy shook her head. "I only wanted to go to the party to see if I could talk to Andrew Nayloss—and he didn't even attend."

"Yeah," Mary replied. "But your date was a disaster!"

"Sure," Lucy replied. "But now I *know*—if I'd gone to the homecoming party, it may have taken me weeks to discover that Andrew Nayloss is really no loss."

They both had a good laugh.

After a while, Matt joined them at the table. Simon reappeared minutes later.

"Hey," Mary said to Simon. "I thought you were going to call Deena."

Simon frowned. "She won't talk to me."

"Neither would I if I were her," Mary told him.

"Yeah, well," Simon replied, "I was caught up in the moment."

"No," Mary shot back. "You were just *caught*."

Lucy got up and brought them some cookies. Simon poured them all glasses of milk. For the next few minutes, the four of them munched cookies and talked.

"So," Matt said between bites, "do you think Uncle Hank and Aunt Julie will have a boy or a girl?"

"Either way is fine," Mary said. "At long as it doesn't have two heads—it will be our *cousin*, you know."

"Well, all I'll say is, if Julie and Hank have a boy, I hope it doesn't turn out like Andrew Nayloss. You wouldn't believe my date," Lucy said.

"What was so bad about him?" Matt asked.

Lucy rolled her eyes. "I had to drive over there and pick him up, open doors for him, pay for everything, and be grilled by his father!"

Matt and Simon exchanged glances.

"Welcome to our world," Matt said.

The phone rang and Matt got up to answer it. "Simon, it's for you," he said. "It's Deena."

Simon brightened immediately.

"Will wonders never cease?" Mary observed. Simon ran to the phone and talked for a long time. When he was done, he came back to the kitchen table.

"Okay," he said. "Who wants to drive me over to Deena's?"

"Hello?" Matt said. "We're having a baby here."

"Yeah, right," Simon said. "I almost forgot."

"Pretty cool, huh?" Matt said. "Today a new life is born right here in our house, but yesterday—just because you read a depressing book for English class—you were Mr. Doom and Gloom."

"Yeah!" Mary added. "The Master of Disaster."

"The Deacon of Depression," Lucy cried.

"The Grim Reaper of Glenoak," Matt threw in.

"Enough!" Simon yelled, covering his ears. "You've made your point."

"You know what?" Mary said. "We haven't heard any screaming for a while."

Just then, they heard their parents cheering upstairs.

Matt jumped to his feet and saluted. "I believe the baby has landed," he said.

Ruthie came trotting into the room. "She had it."

"Boy or girl?" Mary and Lucy said as one.

Ruthie shrugged. "How should I know? I'm just glad she didn't have it in *my* bed."

Upstairs, they heard the sound of a new-born's sobs.

"What do we do now?" Mary asked, scanning the faces around the table. Lucy shrugged. Simon did too. Matt sat back and stretched.

"Who wants ice cream?" Ruthie asked. When nobody responded, she held up her twenty. "I'm buying!"

"Let's go," Lucy said. "But I'm not driving."

"Yeah," Mary shot back. "If you got stopped, you wouldn't want to show anyone your license."

Lucy gave her sister a look, then nodded. "You're right."

"Drop me off at Deena's on the way," Simon said. "I think she's finally forgiven me."

"I wouldn't," Mary said.

"Point taken," Simon replied.

"So," Mary said, putting her arm around Simon's shoulders, "what do you want me to do with Diane Hardt's phone number?"

"Burn it."

Matt got up and opened the back door. He held it as each of his siblings went through. Then he closed the door behind him.

CHAPTER FIFTEEN

WHAT BIG BROTHERS ARE FOR

Reverend and Mrs. Camden rushed down the stairs and into the kitchen. He was faster and burst into the room, arms wide.

"It's a—"

"Empty kitchen," Mrs. Camden said, coming up behind him.

They both shook their heads. "I can't believe they left," Mrs. Camden said.

"It doesn't matter," Reverend Camden replied, taking her in his arms. "I'm excited enough for everybody."

"I'm hungry," Mrs. Camden announced, looking at her husband. "Some of us didn't have any dinner."

Then Reverend Camden had a revelation. "Hey, you know what? This is the first time either one of us has ever been an uncle or aunt—"

"Oh, my gosh!" Mrs. Camden cried. "I'm Aunt Annie!"

Hank sat on the bed next to his wife. They both gazed down into the face of their new daughter.

"We did it," Julie said.

"We sure did," Hank replied, pulling her close. "I'm so proud of you. You were just amazing."

Julie made a face. "Don't be stupid." Then she smiled down at her little girl. "What should we name her?"

"Julie is a beautiful name," Hank said.

"Julie Junior?" She shook her head. "Bad idea."

Hank raised his finger. "Unless, of course, she wants a career as a country-western singer."

Then Julie smiled. "We could name her after Eric and Annie."

"How about Erica?" Hank said.

"Erica Camden-Hastings," Julie sighed. "Perfect."

* * *

Downstairs, Reverend Camden and his wife both jumped when the doorbell rang. "Don't answer it!" Mrs. Camden cried.

"Don't worry," Reverend Camden said. "I'm calm, strong, and capable of handling any challenge." He opened the front door.

The paramedics stood on the porch. They looked embarrassed.

"We would have been here sooner," one of them said. "But we had the wrong address."

"They're upstairs," Reverend Camden said, pointing.

"And mother, father, and baby daughter are all doing just fine," Mrs. Camden called after them as they rushed up the stairs.

"Okay, everybody out!" Matt said. Mary, Lucy, Simon, and Ruthie hopped out of his Camaro and headed for the door of the ice cream parlor.

"Are you sure you can afford this?" Matt said.

Ruthie nodded. "I lost a friend today," she said. "But I can make up for it by eating lots and lots of ice cream."

Matt looked down at his little sister.

He could tell she was sad.

"You know, Ruthie," Matt said, kneeling in front of her, "you may have lost a kitten tonight, but you gained a brand-new cousin."

"Huh?"

"Aunt Julie and Uncle Hank's little baby…that's your one and only cousin!"

Ruthie's face brightened. "Wow! I never thought of it that way."

"Well, you better start thinking of it that way," Matt told her. "Because being a cousin is a big responsibility. Pretty soon, that little kid is going to be looking up to you. In a few years, that kid will want Cousin Ruthie around to show her the ropes."

Matt winked. "Take that responsibility seriously," he said. "You don't want your new cousin to ever be alone."

Ruthie pondered Matt's words for a moment. Then she smiled a smile that was a mile wide.

"Now, *Cousin* Ruthie," Matt said, taking her hand and leading her into the ice cream parlor, "what flavor do you want?"

DON'T MISS THESE
7TH HEAVEN BOOKS!

There's always a beginning...

With a "Meet the Stars" bonus section and 8 pages of color photos!

NOBODY'S PERFECT

Matt has his eye on a new girl, Lucy's trying out for cheerleading—with Mary trying to stop her— Simon's attempting to become invisible, and Ruthie's scrambling just to keep up. Welcome to America's favorite TV family!

MARY'S STORY

Big sis Mary seems to have it all together: She's practical, super-smart, beautiful, vivacious, and a rising star on her school's basketball team. But beneath her perfect exterior, sixteen-year-old Mary is struggling to figure out boys, friends, parents, and life in general—not to mention her younger sister Lucy!

Available wherever books are sold!

ISBN: 0-375-80332-7

MATT'S
STORY

As the oldest kid in the Camden clan and a college freshman, handsome eighteen-year-old Matt often bears the burden of playing referee between his siblings and his parents. Sometimes it's tough to balance family loyalty against a fierce desire for independence, but Matt has earned his reputation as the "responsible one"—*most* of the time.

Available wherever books are sold!
0-375-80333-5

RIVALS

For better or for worse, Mary and Lucy Camden have one thing in common: They're the oldest sisters in a *huge*, busy family! But sometimes the two of them hardly seem related: Strong, independent Mary hangs out on the basketball court, while sensitive, impulsive Lucy loves the mall. And when there's a cute guy involved, it's all-out war!

MIDDLE SISTER

Sometimes being the middle girl in a big family is a tight squeeze—just ask Lucy Camden! It can be kind of tough when your older sister is a beautiful, popular basketball star and your adorable younger sister has a knack for getting her own way. Dealing with brothers isn't always easy, either. But Lucy is her own person and she's determined to stand out—no matter what!

Available wherever books are sold!
ISBN: 0-375-80336-X

MR. NICE GUY

Simon Camden never gives up. When he wants something, he goes for it, no matter how much work (or begging!) it takes. Sometimes his brother and sisters get in the way, and often he feels as if his dog, Happy, is the only one who understands him. But despite his ambition, Simon is the first to help anyone in distress, even if it means putting some of his big plans on hold...

ISBN: 0-375-80338-6

SECRETS

Nothing but the truth...

Everyone in the Camden household—maybe in the whole world—knows when something is troubling Lucy. She's always been the first in the family to speak up—until now...

DON'T MISS THIS BRAND-NEW, ORIGINAL 7TH HEAVEN STORY

Coming February 2001...

LEARNING THE ROPES

Lucy goes to Washington! Her student court group has a date to be shown around the nation's capital for an entire weekend by an important politician. But she quickly learns that politicians aren't always that easy to get hold of. In the meantime, Simon wants to be an entrepreneur, so he decides to baby-sit for one of Ruthie's friends. But once Ruthie finds out Simon's plans, it seems Simon will have one more unexpected kid to look after...

Available wherever books are sold!
ISBN: 0-375-81160-5